6-

THE GUNSMITH

449

The Girl Nobody Knew

THE GUNSMITH

449

The Girl Nobody Knew

J.R. Roberts

SPEAKING VOLUMES, LLC
NAPLES, FLORIDA
2019

The Girl Nobody Knew

ISBN 978-1-64540-097-4

Chapter One

Split Rail was an odd name for a town that had no railroad station. But sometimes there was no telling how a town got its name. This was one of those times.

Split Rail was in Wyoming, smack dab in the center of the state. It wasn't a large town, but it was growing, and as Clint rode in, he thought it would be an interesting place to stop for a few days. He liked that it was not showing any of the modernizations many of the West's towns were starting to display. There was no police department, just a small sheriff's office, and the stores were all common ones—mercantile, hardware store, leather goods, cafes. Other, larger towns were starting to feature places like an apothecary, or a soda fountain. Split Rail had plenty of new buildings, but they housed old-fashioned businesses, which suited Clint Adams.

He found a hotel with a sign over the door that just said HOTEL. It looked good enough to him, so he dismounted and went inside. The lobby was empty, except for a tall, thin, young desk clerk wearing a cheap suit with frayed cuffs.

"Can I get a room, young fella?" he asked.

"Sure thing, Mister," the clerk said. "We got plenty. Just sign in."

He signed the register, making no attempt to hide his real name.

"There you go."

The clerk turned the book around and read it.

"Clint Adams?" he asked, excitedly. "The Gunsmith?"

"That's right," Clint said, "but there's no point in spreading that around, is there?"

"Not if you don't want me to, sir."

"I don't," Clint said. "People will know soon enough, won't they?"

"That depends," the clerk said. "How long are you planning to stay in Split Rail?"

"A day or two, is all."

"Well," the clerk said, "somebody's bound to recognize you, sir."

"I'm sure. Where's the nearest livery stable?"

"There's one around the corner at the end of the street. I could take your horse there for you."

"That's all right, I'll do it," Clint said. "He's a little hard to handle. And then I'll be back."

"Yes, sir," the clerk said. "Here's your key. Room five."

"It doesn't overlook the street, does it?"

"No, sir, the alley."

"That's good. I'll see you in a few minutes."

Clint left the hotel, mounted Eclipse and rode around the corner to the livery.

"Jumpin' Jehoshaphat!" the hostler said, when he rode in. "Look at that animal! I ain't never seen his like."

Clint knew he'd be able to count on the older man, because he referred to Eclipse as "he" rather than "it." That was one sure way to win the Gunsmith's confidence.

"I'll probably be here for a day or two," Clint said. "At the hotel around the corner. You take good care of him."

"Oh, I'll do that, sir," the man promised. "What's his name?"

"Eclipse," Clint said, removing his saddlebags and rifle.

"Let's go, Eclipse," the man said, taking the Darley's reins. "My name's Oscar. You and me are gonna get acquainted."

As the man led Eclipse to a stall, Clint turned and left the stable.

***

When Clint returned to the hotel the lobby was still empty. He'd wondered if, when he got back, word would have already spread, but apparently the young clerk had kept his mouth shut, so far.

He exchanged a wave with the young man and took the stairs to the second floor. He found his room, unlocked the door and entered. It was small, but neat and clean. He dropped his saddlebags on the bed and tested the mattress. It was firm.

He sat and took a deep breath, setting his rifle aside. Bouncing on the bed, he realized he needed a woman. He had been on the trail for weeks, spending time alone, looking at the stars at night, and the clouds during the day, staying out of trouble. He hadn't drawn his gun in all that time, but to clean it, and that suited him.

But now he needed some company—the company of a woman, to help him give his mattress the ultimate test.

He rose, walked to the dresser and used the pitcher-and-basin to wash up. The trail dust gone from his hands, face and chest, he took a fresh shirt from his saddlebags and donned it. Next, he ran his palms over his face. He needed a shave, and there was still plenty of daylight left for him to look the town over, and find a barber shop.

He left his rifle and saddlebags in the room and headed for the lobby.

Chapter Two

Rather than receive directions from the desk clerk, Clint decided he would walk around town and familiarize himself with it. During that walk, he came to a barber shop and went inside.

The barber was just finishing with a man who had a wild, flowing beard.

"There you go," the barber said to the man. "Perfect for another month or so."

The man, in his mid-forties, ran his hands through his beard as he looked in the mirror.

"Good job, Lester," he said. "I'll see you next month."

The man paid the barber and left. The barber turned, looked at Clint and laughed.

"His beard will be a wild mess again within days. I've never known a man's hair to grow as fast as his."

"Why don't you have him come back every week, then?" Clint asked.

"I'm workin' my way up to that," the man said. "Now, what can I do for you? Shave? Haircut? Bath?"

Clint hesitated for a moment, then said, "All three."

***

He took the shave and haircut first, then went in the back to use one of the three wooden tubs there. They were large, round and deep. He pulled a chair over and set his holster down within easy reach.

He was soaping his chest when there was a knock at the door.

"Yes?"

"I have more hot water," the barber called.

Clint looked at his gun, then said, "Come on, then."

The door opened and Lester entered, carrying a steaming bucket. Then he closed the door behind him.

"May I?" he asked.

"Go ahead."

He emptied the bucket of water into the tub, thereby heating the contents.

"Do you think you'll need more?" he asked.

"No, that'll do," Clint said.

"You're new in town," the man said. "I'm the only barber in Split Rail, so I pretty much know everybody."

Clint studied the man, who looked to be in his late 30s, tall and lean.

"I rode in today," Clint said. "This place looks interesting. It seems to be resisting the oncoming future."

"Split Rail has no desire to become modern," the barber said. "We like the West, and the way we live. Oh, we have new buildings, even a new church, but we hang onto the old ways that things get done."

"I saw the sheriff's office," Clint said.

"Ah, the jail," Lester sad, "that's probably the oldest building in town."

"And the sheriff?" Clint asked. "Is he the oldest man in town?"

Lester laughed.

"The oldest man in town is the town drunk," he said. "See, we even hang on to that old chestnut. No, the sheriff's in his forties. He's had the job for about five years."

"Any deputies?"

"He doesn't feel he needs any," Lester said. "He seems to be able to get the job done. The people here are a good lot, and we don't usually get many strangers. Most of our people are . . . suspicious of them."

"I'll keep that in mind."

"Naw, you seem okay," Lester said. "That's why I'm talkin' to ya, to get a feelin' about ya."

"Well," Clint said, "now that you've done that, maybe I can finish my bath in private?"

"Sure, sure," Lester said, laughing. "I'll see ya when yer done."

Lester the barber left, closing the door behind him. Clint would have locked it, but there was no lock. So he continued his bath while keeping an eye on the door, lest someone try to open it silently.

When he finished his bath, he got out of the tub, dried off with a large towel, still keeping his eye on the door. The people in Split Rail may have been good people, but Lester also said they were suspicious of strangers. That meant Clint was going to have to be suspicious of them.

But if he continued to walk around town, stop in at saloons and cafes to drink and eat, and talk, then perhaps the suspicions on both sides would disappear.

Dressed, clean and freshly shorn, he went to the front of the barber shop to settle his bill with Lester.

"How about some lilac water?" the barber asked, showing Clint the bottle.

"No, thanks. I'll just pay for what I've had, so far."

"Twenty cents for the shave, forty cents for the haircut, and a dollar for the bath."

"A dollar?"

"It's a huge tub," Lester reasoned, "and I brought you more hot water."

"But you didn't tell me you'd be charging me extra for it," Clint pointed out.

"All right, then," Lester said. "Sixty-five cents for the bath. That makes the total a dollar and a quarter."

"Lester," Clint said, handing the man some money, "here's two dollars. Thanks for everything."

"If you're in town long enough," Lester said, "come back again."

"I'll keep that in mind," Clint promised.

He stepped outside the barbershop and continued his walk around Split Rail.

Chapter Three

Clint stopped in a saloon called The Riverboat. It had part of a large paddlewheel hanging over the front door. Inside, it had the appearance of a large riverboat ball-room.

He stood just inside the batwing doors to look around. At the same time, the patrons who half-filled the saloon looked him over, as well. He then walked to the bar.

"Help ya?" the bartender asked.

"Beer," Clint said, "cold, if you've got it."

"Only kind we do got, Mister," the bartender told him. He set a sweating mug of beer down in front of Clint.

"Thanks."

Clint sipped it, found it as cold as ice.

"You weren't lying," he said. "This is quite a place."

"The boss used to be a riverboat gambler," the bartender said. "When he won this place, he turned it into a riverboat on land."

"Was it a good idea?"

"We do okay," the bartender said. "Gambling starts after dark."

"Is that a law here?"

"Kind of an unwritten one," the bartender admitted.

"I like this town," Clint said, and then thought, so far. He'd only been there one day.

He drank his beer and looked around. Nothing much was happening at that moment, except for men drinking. That wasn't going to help the itch that he had. For that he needed a woman. So he finished his beer, paid, and pressed on.

***

He'd had a shave, haircut, bath and a beer. Next on his agenda was something to eat. It was getting on to supper time when he spotted a café across the street that seemed to be pretty busy. That usually indicated one of two things. Either it was the only restaurant in town, or the food was pretty good. And since he doubted Split Rail had only one restaurant, he crossed over.

He stepped inside the café and stopped to have a look. It seemed to him all the tables were taken.

"Sir?" A waiter spoke to him.

"I was just checking to see if I could get a table," Clint said. "The place looks pretty busy."

"The Mayflower Steakhouse is a very popular place," the middle-aged waiter said.

"Why isn't the name above the door, or on the window?" Clint asked.

"Everyone knows the Mayflower."

"I guess you're right," Clint said. "Can you recommend another place I could eat?"

"No, no," the waiter said, "we don't want to turn anyone away, especially not a visitor. Give me a moment." He started away, then stopped and turned. "What would be your preference, sir? A table in the front or the back?"

"The back," Clint said. "Against a wall, if possible."

"Give me a moment," the waiter said.

Clint waited while the waiter disappeared into the interior of the café, only to return moments later with a smile on his face.

"Come with me, sir," he said. "I have just the table for you."

Clint followed the waiter through the café, past tables of families, couples, friends dining together, as well as men and women dining alone. Finally, they reached a back wall that was well inside the place and away from the front door and windows. Clint was surprised at how far into the building the café extended.

"Your table," the man said, waiting while Clint sat. "And what can I bring you?"

"A steak," Clint said, "since this is a steakhouse, right?"

"Exactly right," the waiter said. "A steak dinner it will be. And to drink? Coffee? Beer?"

"Beer now," Clint said, "coffee later."

"It won't be long," the waiter promised.

Clint sat back as the waiter went to the kitchen. He looked around at the diners near him, noticed how much they were enjoying their food, whether they were eating with others, or alone.

Moments later the waiter appeared with his plate of steak and vegetables, and a huge glass mug of beer. He set them down on the table and stepped back, proudly.

"Eat," he said, "and enjoy. We like to treat our visitors well here in Split Rail and here at the steakhouse."

"Thank you," Clint said. "I can already tell that I'll enjoy it. But . . . before you go, what's your name?"

"My name is Mayfield Briggs," the waiter said. "My family owns this place. My wife is in the kitchen, doing the cooking. My sons go out and shop and hunt for our supplies."

"That's as it should be," Clint said. "I'm starting to like your town more and more."

"Enjoy your meal," Briggs said. "Let me know if you need anything else."

The only other thing he needed after his food was a woman, but somehow he doubted that Mayfield Briggs could help him with that.

Chapter Four

The steak was perfectly prepared, as were the vegetables. In fact, the carrots were the best he'd ever eaten, cooked to the point of almost melting. He washed the meal down with his mug of beer and continued to watch as customers came and went.

At one point, he saw a woman walking among the tables, speaking to some of the diners. Most of them shook their heads and waved her away. As she came closer he saw that she was young, in her mid-20s, with solid features and long, dark hair. Not a pretty woman, but interesting looking, her body fitting her shirt and pants very solidly.

He slowed his eating as he watched her, and eventually she turned her head and caught his eye. She approached his table.

"This place is very full," she said, "and you're alone. They told me I can't have a table and will have to go elsewhere. I've asked some people if I can sit with them, but they refused me."

"It's an odd request," Clint said, "for a stranger to ask to sit."

"I suppose it is," she said, "but I'm very hungry and don't know if I would make it to another restaurant."

"You look like a hearty girl," Clint said. "I'll bet you could make it."

"It's because I'm tall and hearty, as you put it, that I need sustenance," she said. "I don't want to waste away."

"Well," Clint said, "we couldn't have that, could we? So sit."

She looked surprised.

"Really?"

"Yes, really," he said.

She sat across from him, gratefully.

"Thank you."

"Do you have money?"

"Enough for a bowl of soup, I think."

"No," he said, "you'll need more than that. How about a steak? It'll be on me."

"Oh, no, I didn't mean—I'm not begging—"

"I know that," Clint said. "You're not begging, I'm offering."

"Well . . . all right, then," she said. "A steak would be wonderful."

He looked around, saw Briggs and waved the man over.

"Mr. Briggs," he said, "would you bring this lady the same meal you brought me, please?"

Briggs looked at the woman.

"Would the young lady also like beer with that?" he inquired.

"Yes," the woman said, "the young lady would."

"As you wish," Briggs said to Clint. He turned and walked to the kitchen.

"He didn't want me in here," she said.

"Why not?"

"I don't think he thought I was an appropriate customer."

"What's your name?"

"Angela," the woman said, "Angela Brown."

"I'm Clint Adams," he said, "and while you're sitting with me as my guest, you're an appropriate customer."

She smiled, revealing even, very white teeth.

"I'll remember that."

***

When her food came, she began to wolf it down with an incredible appetite. Clint continued to eat his meal, but slowly. They talked and he found out that, like him, she was a visitor to Split Rail, never having been there before.

"Are you here on business?" he asked.

She paused in her eating.

"I'm not really at liberty to say why I'm here," she said. "I hope you understand."

"Not my business," he said. "I understand perfectly." In fact, he was very glad she didn't have some kind of trouble that she wanted his help with.

They continued to eat. When they had made their introductions she had acted like she'd never heard the name Clint Adams, before. Now, as she continued to eat, it was the same. This also suited him.

He timed his meal so that they literally finished eating at the same time.

"Dessert?" he asked.

"If you're having it."

"Pie and coffee," he said.

"That suits me. Apple if they have it."

Once again Clint called Briggs over. The man appeared and ignored Angela. It was almost as if he didn't even see her sitting there.

"Can I help you?" he asked.

"Pie and coffee," Clint said. "For two. Apple and peach, if you have them."

"Comin' up," Briggs said.

When he returned, he set down two pieces of pie and two coffees, in the center of the table. He left it for them to divvy.

Clint took the peach and pushed the apple across to Angela, with one of the mugs of coffee.

"Enjoy your dessert," Clint said.

17

She smiled.

He nodded and put a hunk of peach pie into his mouth.

Chapter Five

After the meal, Clint paid the bill while Angela went outside.

"Thanks for the meal," he said to Briggs. "Tell your wife it was excellent."

"She'll be glad for the compliment."

"Tell me, why wouldn't you give the woman a table?" Clint asked.

"What woman?" Briggs said, and walked away.

Clint stepped outside, found Angela waiting there for him.

"Are you off to take care of your business?" he asked her.

"I'm off to find a place to stay," she said.

"With enough money for soup?" he asked.

"That would probably get me a room for one night," she told him. "Then I'll just have to go from there."

"No," he said, "I have a room, and a large bed."

She looked at him.

"If a bath goes with it, I'll have to accept."

"A bath," he said. "I know just the place."

He took her arm.

***

Clint took her to the barber shop for her bath, and since the door did not lock, he stood guard outside of it. He heard her get into the tub through the door, heard the water as she soaped herself, and then the barber came down the hall with a bucket of hot water.

"Will she want more hot water?" he inquired.

"I'll ask," Clint said. He opened the door a crack. "Would you like the barber to bring in some more hot water, Angela?"

"I would like the water," she said, "but not the barber. Can you bring it in?"

"Of course."

He turned to the barber, took the bucket and said, "Thanks. You can go."

The barber, Lester, nodded and went back up the hall.

Clint opened the door a crack again and said, "I'm bringing in the water."

"Come ahead."

He entered the room, saw Angela in the large tub, sitting with her back against the side, and her arms outstretched to either side.

"You can't pour it in from there," she said.

He approached the tub, and she moved enough so that her solid breasts came out of the water, which seemed to trickle from her hard nipples. Her long, black hair was plastered wetly to her head and shoulders.

He poured the bucket of extra hot water in the large round tub.

"Would you do me a favor while you're here?" she asked.

"Of course. What is it?"

"Would you wash my back?"

She turned over so he could see the lovely line of her back, as it made its way to the crack of her ass. She got to her knees so that even her butt was above the water. Her flesh gleamed invitingly.

He moved to the side of the tub so he could reach her. She handed him the soap and said, "Do a good job."

He soaped his hands until the lather was like a huge white ball, and then ran his hands over her back, her shoulders, the nape of her neck, to her back again, and then down along the line until he was lathering her firm ass. Then he slid one hand down between the cheeks of her butt, washed her bunghole thoroughly, and kept going. He dipped his hands into the water to dispel the lather, then used his wet fingers to caress the lips of her pussy, before sliding his middle finger into her. She gasped and pushed back against his hand, then began to rock on his finger. She continued riding it, rocking back and forth, her breathing coming harder and harder, until her body went taut and ripples of pleasure coursed through her. She endured them silently, and then her body relaxed.

"You did a good job," she said, over her shoulder. "Thanks. I can take care of the rest."

He rinsed his hands, then got to his feet and walked to the door.

"I'll be right outside," he told her.

She turned and spread her arms again, leaning back, smiling. She arched her back so that once again her breasts came above the water. Her lips looked swollen, and her eyes shone brightly. Her brown nipples were still very hard, and aureoles very wide.

"I feel safer, already," she said.

He stepped outside.

***

Later the door opened and she stepped out, her flesh gleaming, her hair still wet.

"That was wonderful," she said.

"Can I do anything else for you?" he asked.

"Yes," she said, "you can show me that big bed you told me about, so we can finish what we started in the bath."

Chapter Six

They walked together to Clint's hotel, across the lobby and up to his room. He found it odd that no one on the street, or in the lobby, seemed to be looking at them. Angela may not have been a beautiful woman, but she was a striking figure, and he would have thought that the two of them walking together would have attracted attention.

Once they were in his room, the door closed and locked, she turned and rushed into his arms. They kissed, her mouth avid on his, hungry. Her body was solid against his, and promised everything a man could want.

They moved toward the bed and began undressing each other. The gunbelt went onto the bedpost, and then they tumbled onto the mattress together.

"You were telling the truth," she said. "It's big, and it's firm."

He wanted to tell her that so was she, but he was afraid she might not take it the way he meant it, as a compliment. So instead he began to explore her body with his hands and mouth. She smelled fresh and clean from the bath, and parts of her were still moist.

As his face nestled down between her legs and his tongue probed the damp hair, she reached down to hold his head there.

"Yes," she said, "oh yes. I would have had you do this in the bath, but I was afraid you'd drown."

As her pussy grew wet beneath his mouth and tongue, he thought that he still might.

She squeezed his head between her strong thighs as once again ripples of pleasure flowed through her body, and then she implored him to crawl up onto her and enter her. He gave her what she wanted, driving his hard cock into her wet depths, and fucked her hard and fast until he finally erupted inside of her . . .

***

They laid together on the bed a long time before she lifted her leg over him and, wordlessly, mounted him. What was there to say? What words were necessary when he could feel how wet her pussy was as she slid down on his semi-erect cock. Once he was inside her, he swelled to bursting and she began to bounce up and down on him. He watched as her breasts bounced, and she finally leaned forward so he could take her nipples into his mouth. And when her time came, she dropped down on him, stopped, started grinding, her pussy gripping him as her insides spasmed over and over again . . .

***

They dozed, and when he woke, she was still lying on top of him. She seemed to sense that he was awake, and began to kiss his neck, his chest, his belly, until she had kissed her way down to his penis.

"I owe you," she said, and took him into her mouth. When she had ridden him to her finale, she'd released him from her hold without letting him finish. She intended to take care of that now.

As her head bobbed up and down and her lips caressed his hard cock, she suddenly dug her nails into his thighs.

"Ow!" he yelled, "Whoa, Jesus!" He reached down to grab her wrist. "What are you doing?"

"Don't you like a little pain with your pleasure?"

"That all depends," he said. "It has to come naturally, not deliberately. That's not something I've ever wanted to experience."

"Then I'm sorry," she said, rubbing her hands up and down his thighs, "let me make it better . . ."

She held the base of his cock with one hand while the other fondled his testicles, and every so often she released

25

him so she could lick him up and down, and then take him into her mouth again. He settled back, satisfied that she was now making up for the pain. She knew what she was doing, a woman very comfortable with her body, and very knowledgeable about what to do in bed.

In addition to that she had no qualms, no apparent boundaries, as at one point she released his cock, slid her hands beneath him to cup his ass so she could lift him from the bed and lick his anus.

"Jesus," he said, as he almost exploded right then and there, but she gripped his cock tightly around the base again, cutting off any chance of completion on his part. Then she took him into her hot mouth again and finished him that way, causing him to bellow loudly for anyone in the vicinity to hear . . .

***

Later they dressed and went out for supper, for they had been in his room a long time, and had built up an appetite.

Instead of going to the same steakhouse, they found another, smaller place and ate there among mostly empty tables. The middle-aged waitress smiled at them, was very pleasant, and brought them whatever they wanted, telling them there was no menu, and no specialties.

"Just tell me what you want and the cook will make it," she assured them.

So Clint asked for a large bowl of beef stew, while Angela asked if they had any lamb.

"We do," the waitress said. "Not many people ask, but we do."

"A rack of lamb, then," Angela said, "because, for some strange reason, I'm starving."

As the waitress went off to get their orders, Clint laughed, because he knew why.

He felt the same way.

Chapter Seven

After supper they walked the town, until it started to get dark.

"A drink?" he asked her.

"It's been a long day," she said. "Is your offer to spend the night still open?"

"Of course," he said. "Why wouldn't it be?"

"Most men would be happy with what they had already gotten," she told him.

"That wasn't part of the offer," he said. "It wasn't a condition."

"No," she said, "it was something I wanted."

"And you got it," he said. "Now all you need do is come to my room and sleep."

"Sleep," she said, her eyes suddenly fluttering.

"Come on," he said, taking her by the shoulders, "let's go."

So they walked back to the hotel, and even before he got her through the door, it seemed as if she was asleep. He laid her on the bed, undressed her, and covered her with the sheet. Then he sat on the bed next to her and did some reading: Edgar Allan Poe's *The Pit and the Pendulum*.

"What are you reading?" she asked, some time later.

He looked over at her, peering up at him from beneath the sheets. He held the book out to her so she could read the title.

"Poe," she said.

"Have you heard of him?" he asked.

"I have," she said, "but I've never read him."

"He's good," Clint said. "Very dark, but also very good."

"I guess I'm surprised that the legendary Gunsmith reads," she said.

That was the first time she indicated that she knew who he was.

"Why wouldn't I?" he asked.

"It's not part of your reputation," she said.

"Neither is eating or sleeping, but I do both," he said. "I like to sit in my room and read."

"Better than spending time in a saloon?" she asked. "Drinking, and gambling, and having a good time?"

"I used to like doing that very much," he said, putting the book down. "Then men began forcing me to kill them, just to prove a point."

"What point did you want to prove?" she asked.

"It wasn't me," he said, "it was them. They wanted to prove they were faster than me."

"But they weren't."

"No," he said "none of them. Not yet."

29

"But someday, someone will be?"

"Yes."

"So you stay in your room," she said, "to keep from killing, or being killed?"

"There's no way I'm going to keep from being killed," he said. "It'll happen, eventually. There's no point in hiding from it."

"So then," she said, "you do this because you really like to read?"

"I do."

She closed her eyes.

"I'll have to try it, sometime."

In the next minute, she was asleep.

***

Later still, he closed the book and set it aside, then quietly undressed and got underneath the sheet next to her, on her right, so that his own right arm would be free.

He woke later with her sleeping, her head on his shoulder, his left arm beneath her. His right arm was still free, still ready to draw the gun from the bedpost if the need arose.

He fell asleep.

***

In the morning he woke as she rolled off of him and got to her feet.

"What time is it?" he asked.

"Early," she said, "very early. I have to go."

She started to dress.

"You have to get to that job you have to do?" he asked.

"There are things to be done, yes," she said. She turned to him, fully dressed. "But let's meet later, for breakfast."

"Where?" he asked.

"The place we met," she said. "The steakhouse."

"All right," he said. "Will your work be done by then?"

"By then" she asked. "I'll be ready to leave Split Rail. Will you?"

"I don't know," he said. "It's a nice, quiet place. I may not be ready to hit the trail, again."

"Well," she said, "we can talk about it later." She walked to the bed and kissed him. "Thank you for everything."

She turned and left the room. In moments, he had fallen back to sleep.

Chapter Eight

Clint woke later than he'd intended. Since his room's window looked out at the alley, the sun hadn't streamed in and woke him. And his day and night's exertions with Angela had worn him out.

He sat up in bed and swung his feet to the floor. His body was covered with the scent of her. He didn't mind, but knew he'd have to wash it off to start the day. He stood up, walked naked to the dresser, then poured water from the pitcher into the basin.

He washed off as well as he could, not wanting to take the time that morning for another bath. Angela had promised to meet him for breakfast at the café where they'd met, the Mayflower Steakhouse. He hoped he hadn't gotten up too late.

He dressed, strapped on his gun, and left his room. Wondering if Angela might have left him a message, he checked with the desk clerk.

"Any messages for me?" he asked.

The clerk checked and said, "No, sir."

"I thought the woman who came to my room with me might have written one this morning, as she left."

"Woman?" the clerk said. "I didn't see a woman, sir."

"That's all right," Clint said. "Thanks."

As he walked across the lobby, he wondered if the clerk meant he hadn't seen Angela leave, or that he hadn't seen her come in with Clint last night?

He went out the door and headed for the Mayflower.

***

As he approached the steakhouse, he saw that the front door was closed, and there were no customers sitting in the window. Possibly, they didn't open for breakfast. Or perhaps they simply hadn't opened, yet.

He stepped up to the front door and peered inside. He saw Mayfield Briggs moving about, preparing the tables for the day's business, so he assumed they'd be opening soon.

He turned and looked up and down the street, didn't see any sign of Angela Brown. He wondered if Brown was her real name, or if even Angela was. But what would her reason be for giving a false name? Would it have anything to do with why she was in Split Rail? The business she had to conduct?

He heard the door behind him unlock, and turned to see Mayfield Briggs standing in the doorway.

"Good morning, sir," Briggs said. "Will you be joining us for breakfast?"

"I will," Clint said.

"Same table?"

"Please."

"Would you like to come in now?"

"I'm waiting for a friend," Clint said. "I'll give her a few minutes."

"Just let me know when you want to sit," Briggs said.

Clint nodded and Briggs went back inside.

***

Diners walked past Clint into the steakhouse while he continued to wait to see if Angela would meet him there. Finally, his hunger overcame him and he went inside. Briggs showed him to his table, and took his order.

"Steak-and-eggs, of course," Clint said. "And strong coffee."

"And my wife has made some wonderful biscuits," Briggs told him. "I'll bring a basket."

"And plenty of butter," Clint said.

"Of course."

When Briggs returned, he carried the basket of biscuits, and a pot of coffee. There were already two mugs on the table, so he filled one for Clint. As the waiter walked away, Clint broke open a hot biscuit and covered it with butter. As he ate it, he continued to watch for Angela.

The woman had impressed him with her energy, her boldness, and her intelligence. He didn't know what her business in Split Rail was, but he was curious.

Briggs returned with a plate bearing a perfectly cooked steak and prepared eggs. Also on the plate were potatoes and, to Clint's surprise, tomatoes.

"My friend may still arrive," Clint said. "When she does, I'll want the same thing for her."

"Whatever you say, sir."

"You'll remember her," Clint said. "She's the woman who sat with me last night."

Briggs shook his head.

"I don't remember anyone sitting with you last night," he said, "but if she arrives this morning, we'll sure feed her well."

Before Clint could ask him what he meant by not seeing anyone the night before, Briggs turned to tend to another table. Surely he couldn't have forgotten a woman as striking as Angela Brown.

Chapter Nine

Though he was waiting for Angela Brown to join him, Clint didn't let that slow down his enjoyment of his breakfast. The steak was so succulent, the blood running from it mixed perfectly with the eggs. And although he'd never before had tomatoes cooked with his breakfast, they were delicious.

Diners came and went, with Briggs being the only waiter. Could it be that he served so many people he wouldn't remember having served Angela?

He finished his breakfast and became convinced that she wasn't going to show up.

"More coffee?" Briggs asked him.

"Yes," Clint said.

Briggs nodded, went to the kitchen and returned with a fresh pot.

"Briggs," Clint said, grabbing his arm as he turned to leave.

"Yes?"

"What did you mean when you said you didn't remember anyone being with me last night?"

"You sat here alone, sir."

"I did," Clint said, "when I first sat I was alone. But later a girl came in, looking for a seat. You wouldn't give her one, until she came to me. Remember that?"

Briggs looked confused, and shook his head.

"I'm sorry," he said, "no, I don't remember a girl."

"When I paid my bill—"

"You were alone," Briggs said.

"Briggs—"

"I have other tables to tend to, sir," Briggs said.

"Yeah, sure."

Clint finished his coffee and watched Briggs work his other tables. Every so often the man looked over at him, and then ducked into the kitchen.

Why would he deny having seen Angela the night before? The more Clint thought about it, the more he remembered how Briggs ignored her the whole time, spoke only to him. What was that about?

Then it dawned on him that the hotel desk clerk had also denied seeing Angela. Although he hadn't directly asked him the question.

He decided to leave Briggs alone for now and see what he could get from the desk clerk.

He called Briggs over and paid his check.

"Hey," Briggs said, as Clint started to leave, "if your friend happens to show up, what do you want me to tell her?"

"That's okay," Clint said. "If she didn't show up by now, she won't. You don't have to worry about it."

"Whatever you say, Mister—"

"Adams," Clint said, "Clint Adams."

"Wait—"

Clint turned at the door.

"The Gunsmith?" Briggs asked. "That Clint Adams?"

"That's right."

Before Briggs could say anything else, Clint walked out.

***

As he entered the hotel lobby he saw the clerk talking to either a guest checking in, or checking out, so he waited. When the guest—checking in, as it turned out—went up the stairs, he approached the desk.

"Can I help you, sir?" the man asked.

"Yes," Clint said, "we spoke earlier about the guest I had in my room last night."

"Guest?"

"The woman I came in with?" Clint said. "Who left this morning?"

"I don't know who you mean, sir," the clerk said, "but if you say you had a guest—"

"No, wait," Clint said. "You were here at the desk when she and I walked in last night."

"I was on duty last night, yes, sir," the clerk said, "and I did see you come back in, but you were alone."

"That's nonsense," Clint said. "What are you trying to pull? You saw her come in with me, and you must have seen her leave if you were here this morning."

"I'm here most of the time, Mr. Adams," the clerk said.

"Then could you have . . . drifted off to sleep this morning, and missed her?"

"No, sir," the clerk said, stiffening, as if insulted, "I don't sleep on the job."

"So you're going to stick to your story, that you never saw her."

"I'm sorry," he said, "but I didn't."

"Are you afraid you'll lose your job because you let me take a woman to my room? Is that something the people of Split Rail would frown on?"

"I don't know how the people would feel," the clerk said, "but I don't really care if you have women in your room, and I wouldn't lose my job."

Clint thought about grabbing the man by the shirt and dragging him over the desk, but he decided to leave that for later.

"Thanks for your time," he said, tightly.

"I'm sorry I couldn't help."

Clint turned and walked out of the hotel.

Chapter Ten

So far the desk clerk and the waiter swore they had never seen Angela. Clint stood in front of the hotel and tried to think of who else he could ask, then remembered that he and Angela went to another restaurant. It was a smaller place, so surely the waitress would remember.

***

"Can I get you a table, sir?" the waitress asked, when he walked in.

Only a few of the tables were taken, and the woman was working alone.

"I'm afraid I'm not here to eat," he said. "Do you have a moment to talk?"

"Of course," she said. "As you can see, there's no rush. What can I do for you?"

"I was here yesterday."

"Yes, you were. You had a bowl of beef stew."

"That's right," Clint said. "And the woman with me had a rack of lamb."

"I'm sorry." The waitress frowned.

"The lady who was with me," Clint said. "Young, tall, attractive. She had the lamb."

"I'm sorry, sir," the waitress said, "but you must be mistaken."

"About what?"

"Well," she said, "we don't serve lamb here."

"Really?"

"And when you were here, you were alone."

Clint stared at the woman.

"Do you know the clerk at the, uh, hotel—the one that just says Hotel above the door?"

"I'm afraid I don't."

"And a man named Mayfield Briggs?"

"No," she said, "I don't know him, either."

"Really," he said, "you work in a restaurant, but you don't know the owner of the Mayflower Steakhouse?"

She smiled grimly.

"I'm afraid we and the steakhouse exist on different levels, Mister," she said. "I can't even afford to eat there."

Clint stared at the woman. He couldn't figure out what reason she would have to lie. Or the others. He could've tried shaking them until they told the truth, but something was going on. He'd save that approach until later.

"Okay," he said, "thanks for your help."

"I'm afraid I wasn't much help, at all," she said.

"Actually," Clint said, "you were."

***

Clint left the small restaurant and walked slowly back toward his hotel. Three people he was sure had seen Angela with him insisted they hadn't seen her, and that he was alone, each time. Either he had imagined her, or they were lying, for some reason.

And Clint didn't imagine things.

He saw the sheriff's office, which was across the street, and abruptly decided to stop in and see the man.

He crossed over and entered the office. It was small, old-fashioned, featuring wooden desk, a pot-bellied stove, and a rack of rifles on the wall. There was another door that probably led to a cell or two. The only thing in the office that didn't look old was the man seated at the desk. He was in his forties, with a dark beard and hair, and stark blue eyes as he looked slowly up at Clint from the wanted posters he was perusing.

"Can I help you?"

"Sheriff," Clint said, "my name's Clint Adams. I arrived in town yesterday."

"Ah, Mr. Adams," the man said, standing. "My name's Patterson, Sheriff Andrew Patterson. Folks around here just call me Sheriff Andy." They shook hands. "Have a seat, please."

Clint sat across from the man, who reseated himself.

"You're not surprised to see me," Clint said.

"It's my job to know who rides into town," Patterson said.

"The clerk at the hotel?"

"You asked him not to tell anyone, but he didn't think that meant me," the lawman said, "did it?"

"I suppose not."

"So what brings you to see me?"

"A disappearing girl."

"Could you be more specific?"

"Do you know a girl named Angela Brown?"

"No," Patterson said. "I assume she's not local?"

"No," Clint said, "but I'm not sure how often she comes to town."

"As far as I know," Patterson said, "never."

"Well, she was here yesterday," Clint said. "We spent the day together. We were supposed to meet for breakfast this morning, but she didn't show up."

"Maybe she changed her mind?"

"That's possible," Clint said, "but today people I know saw us together yesterday are insisting they didn't see her. They're saying that every time I say we were together, I was alone."

Sheriff Patterson sat forward in his chair.

"Maybe you'd better start at the beginning."

Chapter Eleven

Clint told the sheriff everything that he and Angela did, without getting specific about the sex. The man was old enough to draw his own conclusions about that.

"So she left in the morning," Patterson said, "and the desk clerk claims he never saw her?"

"Coming in, or going out," Clint said.

"Could he have fallen asleep?"

"That's what I asked," Clint said. "The clerk got a little offended, said he never sleeps."

"That'd be Harlan," the sheriff said. "He's right, he never sleeps on the desk."

"Okay, so you know him," Clint said. "Maybe you can get the truth."

"I guess I could talk to 'im."

"What about this Mayfield Briggs?" Clint asked. "Do you know him?"

"Sure I do," Patterson said. "I eat there quite a bit."

"And the waitress in the other place?"

"I think I know the café you're referring to," Patterson said. "I've never eaten there, so I don't know any of the employees."

"Well, it's good enough that you know the desk clerk and Briggs," Clint said. "Maybe you can get some answers."

"That's supposing I believe you, though," Patterson said.

"And why wouldn't you believe me?" Clint asked. "Why would I report a woman missing if she wasn't?"

"I don't know you, Adams," Patterson said. "I know the Gunsmith's reputation, but I don't know for sure that you're the Gunsmith." He raised a hand to ward off any objection from Clint. "Bear with me. Even if I believe you are the Gunsmith, according to your reputation, you might be looking for this woman to put a bullet in her."

Clint stared at the man.

"This is a strange town," he said, finally. "Why would anyone claim to be me if they weren't? That paints a target right on a man's back. I carry that around with me all the time."

"True enough," the lawman admitted. "I tell you what I'll do. I'll ask some around."

Clint stood up.

"We can go to the steak house right now and talk to Briggs—"

"No," Patterson said, "I'll do my job alone, thanks." The lawman stood up. "Fact is, I'll be asking questions about this woman, but I'll also be asking about you."

Clint hesitated, then said, "That's fair."

"You go back to your hotel, or get a drink, or go fishin'," Patterson said. "I'll let you know what I find out."

They left the office together, but from there they went their separate ways.

***

It was Clint's first thought to follow the sheriff, but he decided against it. Instead, he let the man do his job. But that left him in a quandary about what to do with himself. Maybe the sheriff's suggestion that he go fishing was a good one.

But Clint wasn't much of a fisherman, unless he was on the trail and hungry. And sitting in his room with a book wasn't appealing, at the moment.

That left only one option.

A saloon.

***

Sheriff Patterson didn't go to the Mayflower Steakhouse, and he didn't go to the hotel to talk to the desk clerk. He went to a man's office that was two blocks from his own office, and knocked on the door.

"Come in!"

As he entered, the man looked up from his desk, and then frowned.

"What are you doing here?"

"Just checkin' in," Patterson said. "You said you wanted to know if the Gunsmith came to see me."

The man sat back and stared at the lawman.

"Well?" he asked. "What did he want?"

Not having been invited to sit, the sheriff remained standing and relayed his conversation with Clint Adams.

"And you're sure it was him?"

"I'm sure," Patterson said. "He made a good point when he asked who would claim to be him if they weren't? You'd have to be crazy to want that bullseye on your back."

"So what are you supposed to be doing right now?" the man asked.

"Just askin' questions," Patterson said.

"Well," the man said, "go ahead and ask. Just keep me informed."

"Will do."

As the sheriff headed for the door, the man asked, "What was that woman's name, again?"

"Angela Brown," Patterson answered. "Do you know her?"

"We're done," the man said, and Patterson left.

Chapter Twelve

Clint stopped at the first saloon he came to after the sheriff's office, rather than return to the Riverboat. It was a small place called The One-Eyed Jack, and there was hardly anyone inside at that early hour. He had a beer at the bar, and kept trying to come up with a plan.

By the time he got to the bottom of his beer mug, he decided the only thing to do was ask some questions, himself. Leaving the waiter and desk clerk to the sheriff, he figured he'd check some hotels and rooming houses to see if Angela had a room, or livery stables to see if she had boarded a horse.

"Another?" the bartender asked.

"No, thanks," Clint said, paying for his beer. "Maybe later."

"Come on back," the bartender said, grabbing the empty mug.

Clint nodded and left, wondering how many hotels and liveries there were in town?

***

There were three hotels, several rooming houses, and four livery stables. He went to all of them, asked about

Angela Brown, described her, and did not get one eyebrow raise of recognition from anyone. As far as everyone was concerned, she didn't exist.

There was always the possibility that Angela Brown had simply left town. That would explain her absence. However, that would not explain why people he knew had seen her were claiming they hadn't.

Was the entire town trying to make him think he had imagined her? He certainly hadn't imagined the things they did to each other in his room.

Late in the afternoon, he ran out of hotels and liveries, and decided to check in with the sheriff to see if the man had found out anything.

***

"I looked for you at your hotel," Patterson said, as Clint entered his office.

"Sorry," Clint said, "I was out."

"I thought you'd be sittin' in your room waitin' to hear from me."

"I couldn't sit still," Clint said. "I tried out your One-Eyed Jack Saloon."

"Not the best place in town," Patterson said.

Clint sat across from him.

"So?"

"I spoke with Mayfield Briggs at the steakhouse, and with your hotel clerk," Patterson said. "It didn't matter. I squeezed them, but they insist they never saw your girl."

"Goddamnit!" Clint said. "What the hell is going on in this town?"

"Now, take it easy."

"How can I take it easy?" Clint asked. "People are lying through their teeth."

"Why?" Patterson asked. "Why would people be lying about seein' her?"

"I don't have any idea," Clint said, getting to his feet, "but whether or not you can help me, I'm going to find the answer."

"Now hold on," Patterson said. "I can't have you goin' off half-cocked in my town."

"I'm not half-cocked, Sheriff," Clint said. "I'm fully cocked and loaded for bear!"

"Adams," Patterson snapped, as Clint headed for the door, "don't go doin' somethin' that's gonna make me toss you into a cell!"

Clint stopped, held back his initial retort, took a deep breath to steady himself, and then said, "You don't have any reason to do that."

"Not yet, I don't," Patterson said.

"And you won't," Clint assured him, turning away from the door to face the man again. "Believe me, I'm not going to start waving my gun around."

"That's good to hear."

"But I am going to keep looking for Angela Brown," Clint added.

"You knew this woman for one day," Patterson said. "What makes you so all-fired anxious to find her?"

"Maybe because people are telling me she doesn't exist," Clint said. "And maybe because she may be in a lot of trouble. Whatever's happening here, I'm going to get to the bottom of it."

"All right, look," Patterson said, "just keep me posted, okay? At some point, if I can help you, I will."

"Thanks, Sheriff," Clint said, deciding to mollify the man as much as possible. "I'll do that."

He left the sheriff's office, determined to do whatever he could—short of getting himself thrown into a cell—to find Angela Brown.

Chapter Thirteen

As determined as he was to find out what the hell was going on, Clint was at a loss about how to proceed as he left the lawman's office. His original idea was to take some people by the front of the shirt and shake them. So maybe that was the way to go.

He decided to start with the clerk at the hotel, who Sheriff Patterson said was named Harlan.

***

The first thing he noticed when he entered his hotel was that the desk clerk was a different man. He thought he recalled Harlan telling him he was always on the desk.

This man was a beefy specimen with arms that stretched the sleeves of his shirt to bursting, and a bullet bald head. He was about five foot eight, built low to the ground and solid.

"Yeah?" he said, as Clint approached.

"I was looking for Harlan."

"He ain't here."

"I can see that," Clint said.

"So then whataya want?"

"I'm a guest here," Clint said. "I think you should have a better attitude."

"You wanna get me fired?" the man asked. "Be my guest. I hate this job. Now whataya want?"

"Where can I find Harlan?"

"Hell if I know," the clerk said. "Why don't you check and see if he's home?"

"I'll do that," Clint said, "as soon as you tell me where he lives."

"I can't do that," the clerk said. "We don't give that out."

"Well then, can you tell me when he'll be working, again?" Clint asked.

"Hell if I know," the man sad. "He was supposed to be here now, and he ain't."

"Is the hotel manager here?"

"He sure is."

"I'd like to talk to him."

The man leaned a beefy forearm on the desk and said, "Yer talkin' to 'im."

***

As tempted as he had been to yank the hotel manager across the desk, he might have had a hard time, given the size and weight of the man. On the other hand, he could

54

have stuck his gun barrel in the man's face and demanded the address, but then he would have to deal with the sheriff trying to put him in a cell.

So he thanked the beefy man for his time and left the hotel.

His next stop was the Mayflower Steakhouse. Peering in the window he saw that Mayfield Briggs was not on the floor. There was another waiter working. He hoped Briggs was in the kitchen, otherwise it was too much of a coincidence that both Harlan and Briggs were not at work.

He entered the restaurant and was immediately confronted by the waiter, a tall, young man with a quick smile.

"Are ya hungry?" he asked. "We got great food."

"I've eaten here before," Clint said. "I know you have good food."

"Can I get you a table, then?"

The place was about half full, but it was getting on to supper time. Soon, all the tables would be taken, like the day Angela had first walked in.

"No, I don't need a table, at the moment," Clint said. "What I need is to talk to Mayfield Briggs. Is he around?"

"Not today," the man said.

"He has the day off?" Clint asked.

"He just didn't show up for work today," the waiter said. "His wife is real mad."

"And where is she?"

"In the kitchen," the man said, "but she don't allow anybody in there."

Clint passed the waiter a dollar and said, "What if you were just, you know, looking the other way? Waiting on a table?"

"Sure, Mister," the waiter said. "It's no skin off my nose."

The waiter turned to talk to some people, and Clint made his way across the floor to the kitchen. As he entered, his nose was assailed by wonderful smells, and his face with the heat of the kitchen. Standing at the stove was a solidly built woman with a net covering her hair and her sleeves pushed up, exposing forearms a longshoreman would have been proud of.

"Mrs. Briggs?"

She turned quickly, a frying pan held in her hand the way an Indian would hold a tomahawk.

"Whataya want?" she demanded. "What're ya doin' in my kitchen?"

"My name's Clint Adams," he said, "and I'm looking for your husband."

Suddenly, her face changed and she put the pan down. She had a lantern jaw and squinty eyes, but now looked meek.

"So you're the Gunsmith," she said. "I heard you was in town, and that you were here."

"Why not?" he asked "The food's wonderful here. You're a fine cook."

He was surprised to see her blush. Her hands were red, raw, with blunt-fingers as she wiped them on the apron around her waist. Then she extended her right hand.

"It's really nice to make your acquaintance," she said.

He shook hands with the woman, felt the strength in that hand. If she wanted to, she could have crushed his in her grip. He figured she ruled the restaurant and her home with an iron grip.

He was hoping his questions wouldn't get her mad at him.

Chapter Fourteen

"I just need a minute of your time to ask a few questions," he said.

"Can I make you a steak while we talk?" she asked.

"Actually, no, I'm not here to eat . . . but I'm going to come back later."

"Then you mind if I keep workin'?" she asked.

"No, go ahead," he said. "I wouldn't want to be the reason something burned."

"Nothin's gonna burn," she said, confidently. "I never burn nothin'!"

"I know," he said. "Your husband told me you were a great cook, and then I tasted your food myself."

"He said that?"

"He sure did."

"You're probably lyin'," she said, "but go ahead."

"Well," he said, "I'm actually here looking for Mayfield."

"The sonofabitch didn't show up to open this mornin'," she complained. "I had to do it myself, and then find somebody to wait tables."

"That's what the young fella outside told me."

"That's my nephew," she said. "I use him sometimes, but he's basically useless."

"Well, I really just wanted to talk to Mayfield, Mrs. Briggs," he said. "Would you know where he is?"

"If I did," she said, poking with a large fork at some meat she had in a pan, "I'd stick him with this fork before I put him back to work."

"Well, is there somewhere he goes to be alone, sometimes?" Clint asked. "Maybe a fishing hole or something?"

"Try the whorehouse," she said.

"What?"

"That's where he goes sometimes."

"I'm sorry—"

"Don't be," she said, her back to Clint so he couldn't see her expression, "it keeps him from wantin' to rut on me."

"Uh, where is the whorehouse, if you don't mind me asking?"

"I don't know," she said, "Ask Russell."

"Russell?"

"My nephew," she said. "Ask him, and then tell him to get his skinny ass in here."

"Mrs. Briggs," Clint said, "I'm sorry if I made you discuss something . . . unsavory."

"Unsavory?" She turned and faced him. "That's a big word for somebody whose reputation is with a gun. You surprise me. I wish my husband knew words like that.

'Unsavory,'" she said again, as if tasting the word. "Yeah, I guess that's what my marriage is." She considered that for a moment before going on. But I love this place so much, so I guess I'm happy enough." Then she frowned. "But I'd be much happier if that bastard would come back to work. You find 'im you tell 'im to come back, you hear?"

"I hear, Mrs. Briggs."

"You can call me Lolly, Mr. Gunsmith," she said, "and it was fine meetin' you."

"It was fine to meet you, too, Lolly," he said, and left the kitchen while she turned back to her stove, where she was happy.

Back out in the diningroom he signaled to Russell to come over to him.

"Yeah? Did Aunt Lolly hand you yer head?"

"No," Clint said, "she was very nice."

"Nice?" The boy laughed. "I ain't never heard nobody use that word to describe my aunt before."

"She just needs to be treated nice," Clint said, "and she'll be nice."

"If you say so, Mister. Is there somethin' else I kin do for ya?"

"Yes, you can tell me where the whorehouse is," Clint told him. "Your Aunt says you know where your Uncle goes, sometimes."

"Which one?" Russell asked.

"What?"

"Well, we got more than one whorehouse in town, Mister—"

"Adams," Clint said, "I'm Mister Adams."

"Well, sir, we got three of 'em."

"Which one does your Uncle use?"

"All of 'em."

"All right, then," Clint said. "You might as well tell me where they all are."

"Well, there's Kate's, and the Blue Flower, and the Henhouse."

"Henhouse?"

"Yep," he said. "That's what they call 'er. 'The Henhouse.'" Russell laughed.

"Russell," Clint said, "which one do you use?"

"Me? I go to the Henhouse, ever since my Uncle took me there on my fifteenth birthday."

"All right, then," Clint said. "Tell me where they all are, and I'll start with the Henhouse."

Chapter Fifteen

Clint tried the Henhouse first, mainly out of curiosity. He had heard many names for whorehouses, but never one as perfect as The Henhouse. He wondered what quality of girls he would find there.

Following Russell's directions, he found his way to the house with no problem. It was a two-story structure with peeling paint and chipped shingles. On the second floor was a balcony, but at the moment there was nobody on it. He approached the front door, tried the knob and found it locked, so he knocked. The door was opened almost immediately by a girl in a filmy nightgown. She was a little blonde with pointy little breasts and a lush mouth.

"You're a little early, honey," she said. "We don't open for a while, yet."

"I'm not a customer," he said.

"That's too bad." She pouted. "You look like a better class than what we usually get."

"Speaking of what you usually get," Clint said, "is a man named Mayfield Briggs here? Or has he been here?"

"Mr. Briggs, from the steakhouse?" she asked. "He ain't been here for a while, honey. He's got that scary wife, but she sure does cook good."

"That she does," he said. "Thanks."

"Come on back soon, honey," she said, and closed the door.

***

Kate's Place was next, and it was Kate who answered the door. She was a 40ish blonde whose impressive curves were starting to go to fat, but she still had an impish look in her blue eyes.

"First customer of the day, baby," she said to him, which answered his question before he even asked it.

"I'd be happy about that if I was a customer," he told her, "but I'm really just looking for a man named Mayfield Briggs."

"Briggs?" she said. "He's the one from the steakhouse, right?"

"That's him."

"He's got himself a scary wife, but boy, she sure can cook," the woman who Clint assumed was Kate said.

"Has he been here recently?" he asked.

"Nah, we ain't seen Mr. Briggs for a while," the woman said. "But listen, I'm Kate. Why don't you come on in, baby, and I'll see if I can't give ya a discount."

"Maybe later, Kate," he said. "I've still got some things to do."

"Well, come back when you can," she said. "we'll be waitin' for ya."

"I'll remember," he promised, and left.

***

The third whorehouse was wide open when he got there. Russell had called it The Blue Flower, and there was a big blue flower painted on the side of the building—the only side that wasn't peeling. Clint thought these places needed to take better care, but like most whorehouses, they probably put most of their money to work on the inside.

He went through the open front door, saw the sitting room where the girls were on display off to his right. There were a few customers in there with them, but none of them were Mayfield Briggs.

A couple of girls looked out at him, but apparently it wasn't their job to greet newcomers. There was a stairway ahead of him, and a woman coming down the stairs spotted him and plastered a smile on her tired looking face.

"Good-morning, sir, welcome to the Blue Flower," she said, starting her spiel. "We have girls of all sizes, shapes and colors for you—"

"Let me stop you right there," he said, holding his hand up. "Do you know Mayfield Briggs?"

"Sure, he owns the Mayflower. What about him?"

"Is he here?"

"No."

"Have you seen him recently?"

"Whataya mean recently?"

"The last day or two?"

"No," she said, "Briggs ain't been here in a week."

"Great," Clint said, "now where do I look for him?"

"You tried the saloons?" the woman asked. "Man with a wife like that's gotta get drunk every once in a while. Although—"

"Yeah," he said, "I know, she sure can cook. Thanks."

***

He finished with the whorehouses, but the tired looking Madam in the Blue Flower had a decent idea, so he decided to start checking the saloons.

And, while he was at it, have a few drinks for himself.

Chapter Sixteen

He started with The Riverboat.

It was getting late in the day, so the saloon was pretty busy. However, he was able to find a place at the bar with no trouble. What he didn't find was any sign of Mayfield Briggs.

"Help ya?" the barkeep asked.

"A beer."

When the bartender brought the beer Clint said, "And some information."

"About what?"

"A man named Briggs."

"He runs the steakhouse," the bartender said. "Whataya want with Briggsie?"

"Is he a friend of yours?"

"No, but he comes in a lot."

"How much does he drink?"

"With a wife like he's got?" the bartender asked. "A lot."

"Has he been in today?"

"Naw, ain't seen 'im in a coupla days."

"What other saloons does he drink in?"

"How many are there in town?" the man asked. "He drinks in all of them."

Clint finished his beer and set the empty mug down on the bar.

"I guess I better keep looking."

He started to leave.

"You might try Jerry Drake."

He stopped and turned.

"Who?"

"Jerry Drake," the bartender said. "Briggsie and Drake are friends."

"And where can I find Drake?"

"Where else? In a saloon."

Clint looked around.

"I suppose he's not here."

"No."

"What's he look like?"

"Like a tree with legs," the bartender said. "You'll never miss him."

"Thanks for the tip."

Clint left the Riverboat and headed for the other saloons, looking for Mayfield Briggs, or a man who looked like a tree with legs.

***

Clint found Jerry Drake drinking at a small saloon on a side street. He was sitting at a table alone in the back, looking morose. And huge.

Clint approached the bar.

"What's that big fella in the back drinking?" he asked.

"That's Drake," the barman said, "he drinks beer."

"Let me have two."

The bartender drew them and put them on the bar.

"He's not a nice fella," he said to Clint.

"He doesn't look armed," Clint said.

"He don't need to be," the man said. "He's that strong. Look, just don't get him mad, okay? I don't need no breakage in here."

"I'll do my best." He picked up the two beers.

"Whataya want with him, anyway?"

"Just answer some questions," Clint said, "about a friend of his."

"He ain't got many friends," the bartender said. "You must be talkin' about Briggs."

"That's right. Have you seen him, tonight?"

"Ain't seen Briggs in a couple of days."

"Okay, thanks."

Clint walked across the partially empty barroom floor to the table where the tree man was seated.

"Drake?" he asked.

The man looked up at him, bleary-eyed.

"Who wants to know?"

Clint held up the mugs.

"The man with the beer."

That seemed to wake Drake up.

"Have a seat," he said.

Clint sat, pushed one of the beers over to Drake.

"Thanks," the big man said. He took a healthy swallow which, if anything, seemed to clear his eyes up. He had a strong jaw, broad-forehead, and his arms were thick. He appeared to be in his 30s.

"What can I do for ya?" he asked.

"I'm looking for a friend of yours," Clint said, "Mayfield Briggs."

"Briggsie?" Drake said. "What for?"

"I've got a few questions for him."

"He ain't at work?"

"No."

"Then he's probably hidin' from that wife of his," Drake said. "She's a scary cow . . ."

". . . but she can cook."

"If you say so," Drake said.

"You've never eaten there? At the steakhouse?"

"No," Drake said, "I usually cook for myself at home."

"You live in town?"

"Just north of town," Drake said, "in a shack. It's all I need."

"And would you know where Briggs is right now?"

"Not if he's hidin' from Lolly."

"And how often does he do that?"

Drake shrugged his beefy shoulders.

"Every so often."

"And you don't have any idea where his hiding places might be?" Clint asked.

"He's got so many," Drake said. "All over town."

"A guess?"

Another shrug.

"You're just gonna hafta keep lookin', friend."

"I see."

Clint looked at the untouched beer in front of him, then pushed it over to Drake.

"Thanks, friend," Drake said.

"Don't mention it."

Chapter Seventeen

Clint found Jerry Drake's shack, north of town.

He wasn't sure if the idea just occurred to him, or if Drake had actually been hinting at it. After all, why specifically tell Clint that he lived north of town?

Clint approached the shack from the back, just in case Briggs was looking out the front window. He saw that there were more than one person's set of boot prints on the ground in the area. He stopped to inspect them, and decided that two men had made tracks, and one set of smaller boots—perhaps a woman's? Although they weren't all that much smaller, and Angela was a big girl.

He was hoping to find either Briggs or Angela in the shack, but when he peered in the rear window, the place was empty. However, the tracks told him he'd had the right idea, it was just too late.

He decided to take a look inside while he was there. No point in wasting the opportunity.

He walked around to the front, tried the door, and found it unlocked. He went inside, closing the door behind him. It was obvious that a man lived there. It was too much of a mess for a woman to put up with.

He looked around, some the remnants of a meal that was probably Drake's, but there were also indications that another person had been there, recently. However, nothing hinted at a woman's presence.

Clint left the shack, feeling sure that Mayfield Briggs had been there for a while. The question was, who was he hiding from, his wife, or Clint?

***

Not being able to locate the hotel clerk or Briggs, Clint decided to try that small café where he and Angela had eaten. If the waitress who had served them was also missing, then he'd be pretty sure something was going on.

When he got to the café he peered in the door and felt elated when he saw the waitress there. He decided to play this carefully, so he entered and waited. When she saw him she came over and smiled.

"A table, sir?"

"Yes," he said, "in the back."

"This way."

She seated him and said, "You've been here before, haven't you?"

"Yes," he said, "with a lady."

She stared at him, then her eyes brightened.

"I remember," she said. "Only a day or so ago."

"You remember the lady I was with?" he asked, hoping he wasn't pushing it.

"Oh, yes, sir," the waitress said. "An attractive woman."

"I wonder," Clint asked, "has she been in again since then?"

"No, I don't think so."

"And you haven't seen her again in town?"

"I'm sorry, no," she said. "Can I get you something?"

"You know," he said, "I don't think I'm hungry now. How about if I come back later?"

He walked to the door and she followed him, apparently not sure what was going on.

"Well, sure," she said. "Whatever you like, sir."

"And what's your name?"

"I'm Nancy."

"Well, thanks very much, Nancy," he said. "I'll see you later."

"I hope so."

"Oh," he said, "and what's the name of this place?"

"Flo's Café," she said.

He went out the front door and headed for the sheriff's office.

Chapter Eighteen

"What's her name?" the sheriff asked.

"Nancy. She waits tables at Flo's Café, over on Hancock Street."

"And who's Flo?"

"That I didn't ask," Clint said.

"And she remembered you were there with this girl you're lookin' for?"

"Angela Brown, yes."

"So you found one person who remembers her."

"Well, not by name, but she described her to me," Clint said. "Yeah, she remembers. Why don't you go and talk to her?"

"I will," Patterson said.

"Now?" Clint asked. "We can walk over there together."

"I don't need help doin' my job, Adams," Patterson said. "Just let me finish what I'm doin' here, and I'll come and find you at your hotel."

Clint looked at the top of the man's desk, which seemed to be clean, at the moment. But the lawman was simply asserting himself, and if Clint wanted this man's help, he'd have to go along with him.

"Fine," Clint said. "I'll see you then."

He turned and left the office.

***

The man looked up from his desk as Sheriff Patterson entered his office. Patterson couldn't remember a time he'd gone there and found the desk vacant.

"What is it?"

"Do you know anybody named Flo?"

"What are you talking about?"

"Clint Adams found a waitress at a place named Flo's Café," Patterson said. "She remembers the girl he was with."

The man sat back in his chair.

"Have you gone and talked to her?"

"I'm on my way," Patterson said. "I figured I'd stop here, first."

"Well," the man said, "you stopped. Now go and get it done."

"Yes, sir."

"And don't make any mistakes!" the man snapped, as Patterson left.

***

Clint went back to his hotel, hoping that finding Nancy at Flo's Café was what he needed to get his answers. The beefy desk clerk watched him cross the lobby to the desk, and then raised an eyebrow at him.

"Any messages for me?" Clint asked.

"Not that I know of," the hotel manager said.

Clint nodded and headed for the stairs.

"Uh, do you have any idea how much longer you'll be stayin' with us, Mr. Adams?" the man called out.

"Not really," Clint said. "I don't have any place else to go, at the moment."

He went up the stairs before the man could ask more questions.

***

Sheriff Patterson entered Flo's Café, a place he'd never been to before. He had passed it often, but was never curious enough to go in. It was just too small.

Many of the tables were empty, so the waitress came right over to him as he entered.

"Sheriff Patterson," she said. "Can I get you a table?"

"Is your name Nancy?" he asked. "Or are you Flo?"

"There's no Flo," she said. "I'm Nancy. What can I do for you?"

"You can come with me," he said.

She frowned, not sure if this was a request, or some kind of order.

"I can't just leave work—"

He cut her off by taking hold of her arm tightly, and saying, "Now!"

***

Clint sat for an hour, then decided he had waited long enough. He left his hotel—under the baleful eye of the hotel manager—and walked to Hancock Street. As he entered Flo's Café, he saw a middle-aged portly man trying to carry a tray of food across the room to a waiting couple. At one point it looked like he was going to drop it, but he managed to set the plates down on the customers' table—the only table occupied, at the moment.

"Table?" he asked.

"No thanks," Clint said. "I'm looking for the waitress, Nancy?"

"So am I!" the man said. "Without her here I have to cook *and* wait tables."

"Tables?" Clint asked.

"Well," the man relented with a wave, "when there's more than one."

"Are you Flo?" Clint asked.

"Flo was my mother," the man said. "She died several years ago, and left me . . . this." He waved his arms.

"All right, but . . . Nancy was here an hour ago."

"And then she wasn't," the man said. "I came out of the kitchen and she was gone."

"And you didn't see her with anyone?"

"No."

"Can you tell me where she lives?"

"She's a waitress here, not my friend," the man said. "I have no idea."

"Waiter," a man seated at the table called. "This isn't what I ordered."

"Excuse me," the man said to Clint.

"Okay, but if your name's not Flo," Clint asked, "what is it?"

Floyd," the man called over his shoulder.

Clint stepped outside. Now Nancy was gone. Did this happen before the sheriff arrived, or after? And was he a fool to have even thought about trusting the lawman?

Chapter Nineteen

Clint's first thought was to confront the sheriff, ask the man if he had been to see Nancy. If he did that, however, and Patterson was the reason Nancy had suddenly vanished, he would lie.

So his second thought was to follow the sheriff, see where he went, and who he talked to. But to do that he'd have to find him, then tail him without being seen. And he would have to do it himself, as there was nobody else in town he could trust.

Or was there?

In every town there were usually men who would hire out for any kind of work. Usually, they operated on the wrong side of the law, and more often than not would do anything for money.

He decided he needed to find one of those men. There was no longer very much that he could do alone.

Instead of seeking out the sheriff, he changed direction and went to the Riverboat Saloon.

***

"Back again," the bartender said, as Clint found a spot at the crowded bar. "Beer?"

"Definitely."

When the bartender set the mug down in front of him he asked Clint, "Anythin' else?"

"Yes," Clint said, "I'm looking for a man."

"What man?"

"I don't know," Clint said. "A man for hire."

"Ah," the bartender said, "what's the job?"

"The kind that people on the right side of the law wouldn't do."

"Ah," the barman said, again. "But . . . you're the Gunsmith, aren't you?"

"That's right."

"So you want somebody who can use a gun, and who's not afraid of the law."

"Exactly."

"And you're gonna pay him?"

"I am."

"What about me?"

"I can give you a . . . finder's fee," Clint said, "if the man turns out to be what I want."

"Oh, he will be," the bartender said. "But first . . . have you asked around anywhere else?"

"No," he said, looking around, "I thought this was the place to come."

"And you were right."

"So what's his name?"

"Frank Jeffrey."

"And where can I find him?"

"Here."

"Now?"

The bartender nodded.

"But you should know somethin'."

"And what's that?"

"At some point during your . . . arrangement," the barman said, "he's gonna want to try you. After all, you are the Gunsmith."

"What's your name?"

"Hank."

"Hank," Clint said, "he can try me if he wants, after we've finished with my little job."

Hank studied Clint for a moment, then said, "Wait right here."

Clint drank his beer while the bartender came around from behind the bar and disappeared into the crowd of patrons. Some of them looked at Clint with interest, some of them deliberately looked away. After a few moments Hank came back.

"Come with me," he said.

Clint followed the bartender, taking his beer with him. They crossed the room, this time the crowd moved out of their way, until they came to a table with a single man seated at it.

"Hank," the seated man said, "bring us two fresh beers."

"Sure, Frank."

Frank Jeffrey looked up at Clint and said, "Have a seat. I understand you have a job to offer me."

Chapter Twenty

Frank Jeffrey looked to be in his late thirties, wearing trail clothes, a gun and holster on his left hip, an unkempt beard and thick head of hair beneath a battered hat.

Clint sat across from him.

"That's right," Clint said. "I'm looking for a girl who's vanished. And some other people who seem to have disappeared, as well."

"And why do you need me?"

"It looks to me like the sheriff's involved," Clint said.

"What makes you think that?"

"I went to him for help," Clint said. "After I did, one of the people I'm talking about went missing."

"I'm gonna need more," Jeffrey said, "before I decide to work with you."

"*For* me," Clint said.

"I'm not cheap," Jeffrey said.

"I can see that."

Jeffrey laughed.

"I don't spend money on clothes," he said. "Come on, give me all of it."

Hank appeared with their two beers, and over the drinks Clint told Frank Jeffrey the story . . .

***

"That's mighty interestin'," Jeffrey said, when Clint finished. "And I do know Briggs and Nancy, the waitress. I've eaten in Flo's. I don't know the hotel clerk."

"And the girl, Angela?" Clint asked.

"Never heard of her," Jeffrey said. "You must be right about her not bein' local."

"And Drake?"

"Oh sure, I know Drake. We don't get along, but I know him." Jeffrey finished his beer and sat back in his chair. "So what do you think I can do for you?"

"I think the sheriff went to see Nancy," Clint said, "and then she disappeared. I was going to confront him, decided to follow, instead."

"He'd spot you," Jeffrey said, "After all, you're . . . well, you."

"Would he spot you?"

Jeffrey grinned.

"Not if I didn't want him to."

"Then I'd like you to tail him," Clint said. "See where he goes, who he sees."

"For how long?"

"The rest of today, and tomorrow," Clint said. "If he's holding any of these people somewhere, he'd have to check on them. And if he's working for someone, he'll have to check in with them, as well."

"There's one man he might be workin' for," Jeffrey said.

"Who's that?"

"Let me watch him, first," Jeffrey said, "see if I'm right. Then I'll tell you."

"Okay."

"Now comes the question of payment."

"How much do you want?" Clint asked.

Jeffrey looked surprised.

"You don't want to dicker?"

"I don't have time."

Jeffrey gave it some thought.

"Fifty dollars a day."

Clint didn't give it any thought, at all.

"Okay."

"And expenses."

"Done. I'm staying at the—"

"Everybody in town knows where you're stayin'," Jeffrey said, cutting him off.

That wasn't something Clint wanted to hear.

"Well then, come and see me tonight, let me know what you've found out, so far."

Jeffrey stood up. He was taller than he had seemed while seated.

"I'll get right on it."

He walked across the room and out the batwing doors.

Clint walked back to the bar with the two empty beer mugs, set them down. Hank came over.

"Another?" Hank asked.

"No," Clint said. "I think I got what I came for." He pushed five dollars across the bar. "Finder's fee."

"Thanks," Hank said, pocketing the money.

"Can I trust him?" Clint asked.

"Why do you ask that now?"

"I never knew a left-handed man I could trust," Clint said. "And he agreed pretty quick."

"You can trust him as long as you're payin' him," Hank said, "and for as long as you got somethin' he wants."

"Like?"

"A reputation."

"It's not all it's cracked up to be," Clint said.

"Most men got to find that out for themselves," Hank said, "don't they?"

"They sure do," Clint said, "and most of them do it the hard way."

Chapter Twenty-One

As he left the Riverboat Clint now felt he had the sheriff covered. He was taking a chance trusting Frank Jeffrey, a man he didn't know, but he felt he knew the type. As long as the man stayed interested, he would be able to count on him.

Clint felt his own next move had to be to try to find Briggs, or the desk clerk from the hotel. If they weren't being held, maybe they were in hiding. It certainly seemed as if Briggs had been hiding in Drake's shack. That meant that perhaps Drake could lead him to Briggs. With Jeffrey following the sheriff, that left Clint free to follow Drake. Or perhaps the beefy hotel manager could lead him to the desk clerk.

He decided to start at his hotel.

***

As he entered the lobby the desk clerk looked up at him and he realized this was someone new. He was a tall, thin man in his 30s, with sparse hair and an even sparser mustache. As Clint approached the desk the man smiled timidly.

"Help you, sir?" the man asked.

"I'm already a guest," Clint said. "My name is Adams."

"I'm sorry, sir," the man said, "I'm new here. I don't know all the guests. Can I do something for you?"

"Are you new to Split Rail?" Clint asked. "Or just new to this job?"

"The job," the man said. "Seems like the regular desk clerk has, I don't know, disappeared."

"And who hired you? The hotel manager?"

"That's right."

"A sort of beefy man named . . ."

"Mike Feeny. He's not only the manager, he owns the place."

"And does he live here in the hotel?"

"As far as I know, Mr. Feeny's got a house in town someplace."

"I see. Well, I hope you enjoy the job . . ."

". . . Lyle," the man said, "my name's Lyle Conway."

"Lyle," Clint said. "Thanks very much."

"Sure, Mr. Adams."

As Clint went to the steps to go up to his room, Lyle Conway opened the register and read his name.

"Clint Adams?" he whispered. "Jesus!"

***

Clint slept fitfully.

One reason was Frank Jeffrey never came to his room to report on the sheriff's movements. He couldn't be sure what that meant. Was the man untrustworthy, after all . . . or was Jeffery now missing?

He woke with his eyes feeling as if they were filled with dirt, as if he had slept on the desert. He washed his face, hoping that would make them feel better. Once he was dressed, he went downstairs and decided to go to Flo's Café for breakfast. He didn't expect to see Nancy there, but you never know.

When he entered, Floyd was waiting on a table with three men seated at it. When he saw Clint he rushed over.

"I'm sorry, but Nancy still hasn't come to work."

"That's all right," Clint said. "This time I'm here for breakfast."

"Oh, well, in that case, take any table you like," Floyd said. "Coffee?"

"Yes, black and strong."

"Comin' up. Breakfast?"

"Eggs," Clint said, "and some bacon?"

"Biscuits?"

"If it's not too much trouble."

"Don't worry," Floyd said "I'm a better cook than I am a waiter. Looks like I might have to hire a new waitress if Nancy doesn't come back soon."

"Too bad," Clint said. "I got the impression she was a good one."

"I thought so, too."

Floyd went into the kitchen. Two other tables were occupied, the one with the three men, and another with a middle-aged woman and a younger one who was probably her daughter. The young one was staring at Clint, then quickly looked away.

Clint had decided to eat at Flo's for two reasons. One, Nancy might be back, and two, he wanted to watch Floyd for a short while. He wasn't convinced that the man was as clueless about Nancy as he claimed to be. After all, why should he be telling the truth when nobody else seemed to be?

Floyd came out carrying a coffee pot, and a mug. He put them on Clint's table, then went back to the kitchen. He returned fifteen minutes later with Clint's breakfast.

"Is the coffee strong enough?" he asked.

"Perfect," Clint lied. "Thank you."

"Enjoy your breakfast."

The three men paid their bill and left, leaving only the two women. Clint took his time eating, and eventually the ladies also left, with the daughter throwing Clint one more glance.

When he was almost finished Floyd returned and asked, "Is there anything else I can get you?"

"I could use some information, Floyd," Clint said. "Why don't you have a seat?"

Floyd looked around. The place was empty, so he had no reason not to sit.

Chapter Twenty-Two

"This place is called Flo's, and your name is Floyd," Clint said. "Coincidence?"

"Yes," Floyd said. "My mother's name was Florence. She's the Flo the place is named after."

That had a ring of truth to it.

"Do you still say you don't know where Nancy lives?" Clint asked.

"It's true," Floyd said. "I don't get personal with the waitresses I hire. They don't last very long."

"Do they usually disappear, like Nancy did?"

"No, this is unusual," Floyd said. "They usually give me some notice."

"I really need to find her," Clint said. "Can you at least tell me if she lived in town?"

"I think so," Floyd answered. "In fact, I think she once told me she only lived a ten-minute walk from here."

"That's very helpful," Clint said. "Thank you."

Two people came to the door and looked around.

"Excuse me," Floyd said. "I have to get them seated before they decide to go somewhere else."

"I understand."

Clint finished his breakfast, paid his bill and left.

***

Clint decided to walk ten minutes in every direction, looking for places a waitress like Nancy might have taken a room. He also stopped in some stores to ask if anyone knew her. He got lucky in a small mercantile.

"Sure, Nancy buys her coffee and candy here," the man behind the counter said. "She lives around the corner, above a hardware store. Can't miss it."

"Thank you."

"You interested in courtin' the gal?" the older man asked, a twinkle in his eye.

"Something like that."

"She sure is nice."

"Yes, she is," Clint said. "Thank you."

He left the store and walked around the corner. The hardware store stood out, as it had barrels and cartons on the boardwalk in front of it. On the side was a stairway going up to the second level. Clint climbed the stairs and knocked. When there was no answer, the door was easy to force, and he did so.

He entered, found a very neat room with a small sofa and matching chair. Against one wall was a stove, with a small table in front of it and two chairs. There was the doorway to another room, and through it he could see a bed. He approached the stove and touched it, found it cold. He checked her cupboard, found it very bare.

He turned, once again looked through the doorway at the bed, then decided to go in. When he did, he both wished he hadn't, and was glad he had. The reason was the same for both.

Nancy was on the floor on the far side of the bed, so he couldn't have seen her from the other room. He knelt beside her to check, and found that she was dead. There were no wounds, but then he saw the marks on her neck.

Someone had strangled her.

Clint sat on the bed and looked down at the body. He remained that way for several minutes. He was wondering if it would do any good to report this to the sheriff. Then the lawman would come here, with Frank Jeffrey following behind, and they would all be in the same place at the same time.

And what was the point? Was the sheriff going to try and find out who killed her? At this point Clint doubted it. It might even turn out to be the lawman who took her from her work place, brought her here and killed her. And if that was the case, why tell the man he had found her? Let him think he was still in the clear.

And there was still Mayfield Briggs and the desk clerk from the hotel to find—hopefully still alive, but considering what he had just found, what were the chances?

He decided to leave and not mention this to anyone. He just needed to make a stop at the small mercantile around the corner.

***

He knew that when the body was found, the clerk at the mercantile was going to remember their conversation. He had some damage control to do.

He entered the store and the clerk, not busy at that moment, immediately smiled.

"You find her?" he asked.

"I found the place, but I knocked on the door and there was no answer."

"You might as well check Flo's Café, then," the man said. "She's probably at work."

"I'll do that." He started to leave, but stopped short. "Do you know the man who owns that place?"

"Floyd? I've met him once or twice. Inherited the place from his mother, Florence. Now, there was a nice lady. And a damned good cook. She died a few years ago."

"Okay, thanks."

The information confirmed that Floyd was being truthful. That was a real rarity in this town.

Chapter Twenty-Three

Clint was shaken my Nancy's death. It might not only make it possible that Mayfield Briggs and the desk clerk were dead, but Angela Brown, as well.

Clint wondered why anyone would want to kill Angela, but then thought, why not? He knew very little about her, didn't know what business had brought her to town. He had been stumbling around in the dark from the beginning, and he still was.

He needed to talk to somebody who definitely knew where one of these missing people were, and the only one he could think of was Jerry Drake.

He started hitting saloons, searching for the man who looked like a tree with legs.

***

After a fruitless search for Drake, Clint went out to the man's shack. There was smoke coming from the pipe on the roof that acted as a chimney. He approached it slowly and quietly. Just in case Briggs was inside.

But as he peered in the window he didn't see anyone inside. He walked to the front door, tried it, found it unlocked and entered. He could smell death immediately, and his heart sunk. Sure enough, off in a corner, where he had been unable to see them from the window, were both Briggs and Drake.

He checked the bodies quickly, saw that they had both been stabbed. Once sure they were dead, he got out of there fast and put some distance between himself and the shack.

***

He did not report their deaths. He was convinced he couldn't trust anyone—not even the man he was paying, Jeffrey. But if Jeffrey would finally report on Sheriff Patterson's movement, Clint might be able to eliminate the sheriff from suspicion in the deaths of Nancy, Briggs and Drake.

And where the hell was the hotel desk clerk—damn, but if he ever heard the young man's name he couldn't remember—and Angela Brown?

He decided he had to find Jeffrey, and that meant finding the sheriff.

He went to the sheriff's office and, after a quick look through the window, determined that he was there. He then looked all around outside the office—across the street, up and down the street, even on rooftops—but did not see Frank Jeffrey.

Too many goddamned people were disappearing.
He decided to simply confront the lawman.

***

He entered the man's office. He was not behind the desk, or even in the room, but sweeping sounds could be heard from the cell. As he closed the door with a bang, the sweeping stopped and the sheriff appeared.

"Ah, Adams," Patterson said, setting the broom aside. "I have to do everythin' around here."

"A lawman's work is never done," Clint said.

Patterson didn't seem to notice the sarcastic edge to Clint's comment.

"You've got that right," Patterson said. "Oh, by the way, I never found that waitress, Nancy."

"Oh no?"

"I talked to the fella who owns Flo's Café, he doesn't know where she's gotten to."

Floyd said he didn't see Nancy with anyone, and he never mentioned the sheriff coming by to ask about her. More and more it was looking like the sheriff was involved in whatever was going on.

Should he tell the man he'd found the bodies? No, not just yet.

"Do you know a man named Jerry Drake?"

Patterson frowned.

"Not by name."

"Big fella, looks like a tree with legs."

"Now that sounds familiar," Patterson said. "Huge, lumberin' man? Drinks a lot?"

"That's him."

"I think I've had him in my cells once or twice," Patterson said. "What about him?"

"He's supposed to be a friend of Mayfield Briggs."

"Really? Have you talked to him?"

"I thought you should."

"That's good thinkin'," the lawman said. "I'll find him right now and question him." He stood up and grabbed his hat.

They stepped out of the office together.

"Nice to see you taking action right away," Clint said to the lawman.

"I told you," Sheriff Patterson said. "I do my job."

"Well," Clint said, "let me know what he says."

"You'll know when I do."

Clint watched the man walk away, wondered if he'd manage to avoid finding the bodies in Drake's shack?

Chapter Twenty-Four

Clint went back to his hotel, found an agitated Frank Jeffrey waiting in the lobby.

"What the hell are you doin'?" Jeffrey demanded.

"What are you talking about?"

"You hired me to follow the sheriff, and then you show up at his office today?"

Clint looked around. They were attracting some attention.

"Let's go to a saloon."

"I don't want a drink—"

"I do!" Clint snapped. "Come on."

There was a hole-in-the-wall saloon right across the street. Clint led the way. He went to the bar, got two beers and carried them to a table where Jeffrey sat.

"Where were you?" Clint asked. "I went to the sheriff's office looking for you. I only went inside when I didn't see you."

"You weren't supposed to see me," Jeffrey pointed out. "Neither was he."

"Where the hell were you?" Clint asked, again.

"That doesn't matter," Jeffrey said. "I saw you go in, and I came here to wait for you, to find out what the hell you're doin'? Do you want me to follow him or not?"

"I do," Clint said. "I wish you were following him right now."

"And are you gonna stay away?"

"Yes, I am."

"Then where is he?" Jeffrey asked. "Where can I pick him up?"

"There's a shack, just north of town," Clint said. "He should end up there."

Jeffrey stood up.

"There's just one thing . . ."

***

Clint had to give Jeffrey some money after he told him about the bodies.

"This better not come back on me" Jeffrey said, "or it's gonna cost you a lot more."

"It won't."

After Jeffrey left, Clint had one more beer, then stepped outside. There was only one person he might be able to locate, not counting the original missing person, Angela herself.

He went back to the hotel, to the desk, where the new clerk was standing.

"Sir?"

"What's the hotel owner's name?" he asked. "The big, beefy guy. Feeny?"

"That'd be Mr. Mike Feeny, yeah."

"Is he here now?"

"No, sir."

"Not in his office?"

"No, sir."

"And you don't know where he lives?"

"No, sir."

"Where's his office?"

The clerk pointed.

"Back there."

"I need to look around for a few minutes."

The clerk shrugged.

"Okay."

"Just okay?"

"You're the Gunsmith, right?"

"That's right."

"So, okay."

Clint went down a hall behind the desk, tried one door, found a storage room, then another door before he found the manager/owner's office.

***

"He told me where Jerry Drake lives," Sheriff Patterson said.

The man behind the desk shrugged,

"So?"

"So, if he was out there, then he knows," the lawman said. "He found the bodies."

"If he found the bodies, why would he send you out there?" the man asked.

Patterson thought a moment.

"To find the bodies?"

"Then go and do your job," the man said. "If you don't find them, then he's going to know for sure that something's amiss."

"Amiss?"

The man rolled his eyes.

"Wrong," he said, "he's going to know something's wrong. Just go and do what you've got to do."

"What I gotta do?"

"Yes."

"Okay," Patterson said, and left the office.

Chapter Twenty-Five

Clint entered the hotel manager's office, found it small, with only enough room for the desk and chair, and a file cabinet. He quickly got behind the desk and started looking at everything on top, then went through the drawers. He was about to switch to the file cabinet when he found what he wanted, a letter addressed to the hotel manager, but not at the hotel. There was another address and that was what he wanted.

Rather than take the envelope and have it missed, he found a blank slip of paper, wrote the address down, and put the envelope back in the drawer.

He left the office, and the hotel, and hoping the fact that he was the Gunsmith would keep the clerk's mouth shut.

***

Frank Jeffrey remained hidden outside of Jerry Drake's shack for a good half hour before Sheriff Patterson appeared. The lawman looked around to see if he was alone, and didn't spot Jeffrey at all. He finally went inside.

Jeffrey left his cover and made his way to the shack so he could peer in a window. He watched as the lawman walked to the two bodies on the floor, as if he knew they were there all along. Betraying no hint of surprise, he simply rolled them over, then stood there staring down at them. Finally, he found two blankets and wrapped them up, then turned and headed for the door.

Jeffrey left his window and rushed back to his cover before Patterson came out the door. As the lawman left the area, Jeffrey was close behind.

***

Clint found the address on the envelope, a small house among other small houses, all in need of some degree of repair. He was assuming the hotel manager lived there. He was also hoping that maybe the man was hiding the desk clerk inside. He didn't know why that would be, but it would certainly be easier if the boy was hiding there.

He started up the walk.

***

Frank Jeffrey followed the sheriff back to town, where the man collected a buckboard from a livery stable. Since Jeffrey had a good idea what he planned to do with the buckboard, he reversed direction and headed back to the shack, so he'd be there when the lawman got back.

Once there he watched as Patterson carried the bodies out and dumped them onto the back of the buckboard. Then the lawman climbed up onto the driver's seat and headed back to town. It was easy to follow on foot, as the buckboard was being pulled by a single horse, and not moving very quickly.

It was going to be interesting to see what he was going to do with the bodies.

***

Clint knocked on the door of the house and waited. He was surprised when it was answered by a handsome-middle-aged woman in a blue dress. Did the hotel manager have a housekeeper, or was the beefy man lucky enough to have this woman as a wife?

"Yes?" she asked. "Can I help you?"

"I'm sorry, Ma'am," Clint said, "but does the hotel manager, uh, Mr. Feeny live here?"

Her face became stern and she said, "He did."

"Did?"

"I'm Mrs. Feeny," she said, "and I threw him out weeks ago."

"Oh, I see. Can you tell me where he lives now?"

"I don't know and I don't care."

"Mmm," Clint said. "Maybe you can help me, then."

Her face softened, became pretty as she said, "Well, I'll sure try. Would you like to come in for . . . a cup of tea?"

"That would be nice," he said, "thank you," and followed her in.

***

The sheriff avoided driving down Split Rail's main street with the two bodies. Instead he took them down a pretty deserted street to a dilapidated barn and proceeded to unload them there. Then he locked the doors, and started off in the buckboard again. Jeffrey followed on foot again but, as he suspected, Patterson was now simply returning the buckboard and horse.

When the lawman came out, he headed into town on foot, with Jeffrey following at a safe distance. The sheriff lead him to Split Rail's main street, where he stopped in front of an office with a shingle hanging in front of it, and went inside.

Jeffrey didn't have to get close to read the shingle, because he knew whose office that was. He figured he now had something to tell Clint Adams that the Gunsmith would find interesting.

Chapter Twenty-Six

"It gets lonely here, sometimes," Louise Feeny said.

"Then why don't you let your husband come home?" he asked.

"Because he's a pig and I can't stand it anymore," she said. "He's not a gentleman, like you."

She smiled and reached out to touch his hand.

"Mrs. Feeny—"

"Louise, please," she said. "And what's your first name?"

"Clint."

"That's a good, strong name," she said. "Do you know what my husband's first name is? Norman! That's why he has everybody call him Mike."

"Louise," he said, "you said you might be able to help me."

"Oh, right," she said, "you're lookin' for someone."

"The young desk clerk from the hotel," Clint said. "He's disappeared and I need to talk to him."

"Well, that'd be Harlan," she said. "He's kind of cute. You know, if I wasn't so much older than him . . . do I look very old?"

"You're a lovely woman, Louise," he said. "You know that."

"And you need to find Harlan, right?" she asked, getting out of her chair, across the table from him. Between them were two untouched cups of tea.

"That's right."

"Well," she said, walking over to stand next to him, putting her hand on his shoulder. "If I do somethin' for you, then you'll have to do somethin' for me."

"I suppose that's fair," he said. "What do you want me to do?"

Abruptly, she slid right into his lap, and put her arms around his neck.

"Let's see if I can come up with somethin'," she said, and kissed him.

***

"You what?" the man behind the desk barked.

"What else was I supposed to do?"

"Where did you put them?"

"In that old barn I keep on Collins Street."

"Is it locked?"

"Of course."

"And nobody saw you?"

"If they did, they only saw me ride in. They don't know what I had."

"What are you going to tell Adams?"

"I've been lyin' to him this long, why not keep goin'?" Patterson said. "I'll tell him I got there and the shack was empty. He's been lookin' for missin' people, now let him start lookin' for missin' corpses."

The man sat back behind his desk and thought about it for a moment.

"You could be right," he said, finally. "That'll keep him busy."

"That's what I figured."

"What about the woman he was looking for in the first place?"

"Still missin'," the lawman said. "I wish she'd come back, then maybe they'd both leave town."

"What was her name?"

"Angela Brown."

The man thought for another moment.

"Still does nothing for me," he said. "All right. Let me know what happens with Adams."

"Sir," the lawman said, standing, "are you sure you don't just want him dealt with?"

"Killed?" the man asked. "Why would we want Split Rail to become known as the town where the Gunsmith was killed. I've got a lot of business to do here, Patterson." He waved a hand. "That's all."

The dismissal stung a bit, but the sheriff turned and left.

***

Frank Jeffrey followed the sheriff back to his office, and then decided to leave him there. Chances were he would be there a while after the past few hours he had. The man needed some rest.

Jeffrey walked back to the old barn where Sheriff Patterson had stashed the bodies.

Who knew what else he had in there?

He tried the padlock on the front door, but the chain and lock were much newer than the rest of the barn. After looking around to be sure he was alone, he walked to the rear of the barn and found another, smaller door. When he put his shoulder to it, the door popped open. A new lock and chain on the front, but the back gave easy access. Sometimes people were so careful, they weren't smart.

He opened the door and stepped inside. First he noticed the darkness, then the smells. There was hay, dust . . . and, predominantly, death.

Chapter Twenty-Seven

The kiss went on for a long time and was quite enjoyable. Her weight in his lap had the desired effect, and she felt his cock harden beneath her. He enjoyed the scent of her, and the feel of her solid flesh against him, but he was also aware that he was kissing another man's wife.

"Mmmm," she moaned, breaking the kiss. "I hope you don't mind me doing this."

"I don't mind," he said. "It's very enjoyable. But you're a married woman—"

"Not for much longer," she said kissing his neck, and his jawline, "I can assure you of that." She wriggled in his lap. "Ah, I feel another part of your body that doesn't mind that I'm married."

"Louise," he said, "I don't have time—"

She slid from his lap to her knees on the floor, and began to undo his trousers.

"Let's make time," she said.

"Louise—" He grabbed her wrists.

"Do you want to know where Harlan is?" she demanded.

"You know I do."

"Then let go of my wrists."

Reluctantly, he did. She continued to undo his trousers until she had his hard cock in her hand. He was uncomfortable, so he removed his gunbelt, put it on the table, then lifted his hips so she could pull his trousers down around his ankles.

Now that he was completely naked from the waist down, she kissed his thighs while stroking his cock with one hand, and fondling his testicles with the other.

"My God, you're a lovely man," she said. "My husband's peter is an ugly, wrinkled thing. You're so smooth . . ."

She leaned down to run her tongue over his smoothness, and from that point on he stopped thinking of her as married.

***

Jeffrey waited until his eyes became adjusted to the darkness in the barn, then looked for a lamp to light. He walked around, holding the lamp aloft until he found an old stall where the sheriff had dumped the two bodies. But these bodies were fresh, and not giving off the smell of death he had detected.

He unfolded the blankets just to satisfy himself that these were the bodies Patterson had removed from the shack, then covered them again.

He began to move around the barn, trying to find the source of the smell that hit him when he walked in. Finally, he came to a seed bin, where the lid looked as if it was ajar. When he opened it, he saw what had to be another blanket wrapped body. He had to move it in order to find the top and unwrap the blanket to reveal a young, male face that had already started to deteriorate, hence the smell.

He didn't know who the young man was, but he had a good idea. He unwrapped it further, just enough to be able to describe what it was wearing. Let Clint Adams make the determination as to who it was.

***

While Frank Jeffrey was dealing with putrefied flesh, Louise Feeny was taking Clint Adams' smooth-fleshed cock into her mouth in one swift move, engulfing it. Clint tensed as she started to bob up and down, sucking him avidly, and then relaxed, deciding to enjoy it, and maybe get it over with quickly, at the same time.

But that wasn't Louise Feeny's plan. After she had sucked him for some time, moaning in appreciation of his taste, smell and feel, she released him from her mouth and stood up.

"Wha—" he said, but as she removed her dress he realized what was coming next.

When she was naked, he saw lots of pale soft skin, a bit of matronly spread to her hips and belly that was not at all unattractive. Clint had a great liking for experienced women, and Louise may not have been happy with her husband's sexual performance, but she herself was quite experienced.

She straddled him, pressing her large breasts to his face, and sat right down on his penis, which was still wet and gleaming with her saliva. As her heat closed around him and she settled into his lap, he put his arms around her and sought out her dark nipples with his mouth.

She grunted and groaned aloud every time she came down on him, the chair he was sitting in creaking, as if it would break at any moment from their combined weight. To avoid that, he slid his hands beneath her butt, gripped it and stood up. Then he set her down on the table, which was a little more solid than the chair.

As soon as her butt touched the table, she fell onto her back. He was still inside her, so he grabbed her legs, spread them and began to fuck her hard and fast, now determined to finish.

"Wait, wait . . ." she said, but it was too late. Her body took her over the edge, right into a pool of pleasure that caused her to shout. Moments later he groaned aloud, and emptied himself into her.

***

"I'm not sure . . ." she said.

"You said you knew where Harlan was," he reminded her.

"Well," she said with a smile as she pulled her dress up to cover her breasts, "I wanted you to fuck me."

"Louise—"

"I'm not gonna apologize," she said. "It was wonderful—over too quickly, but wonderful."

"What if your husband had walked in on us?" he asked.

"Then you would've shot him."

"I would not—"

"Relax," she said, "he doesn't come around here."

"Would he be hiding Harlan wherever he lives now?" Clint asked.

"I would imagine he's stayin' in a room in the hotel, but as for hidin' Harlan, why would he? They're not friends. The boy works for Mike, but they don't get along."

"So you don't know anything?"

"I didn't say that," she said. "There might be something I can tell you that could help."

Chapter Twenty-Eight

As Clint approached his hotel, he heard his name from across the street. He turned and saw Frank Jeffrey. He crossed over.

"What are you doing over here?" Clint asked.

"I didn't want to be seen with you in the lobby," he said. "Just in case."

"What've you got?"

"Something you got to see," Jeffrey said.

"I was just on my way to find the desk clerk, Harlan," Clint said. "I talked to the hotel manager's wife and she hazarded a guess that—"

"Forget about guesses," Jeffrey said. "What's he look like and what was he wearin' the last time you saw him?"

Clint described Harlan, the desk clerk, to Frank Jeffrey.

"I found him," Jeffrey said.

"Where?"

"Come on," the man said. "I'll show you."

***

"In there?" Clint said, looking at the old barn.

"In there," Jeffrey said, "and hold your nose when we go in."

Clint followed Jeffrey to the back door of the barn, and inside. He caught the odor as soon as they entered, but didn't hold his nose. He had smelled death before.

"Damn it," Clint said, "he's dead?"

"Not just him."

Jeffrey picked the lamp up from where he'd left it and lit it. He led Clint first to the stall where two bodies were.

"Those the same bodies you found?"

Clint moved the blankets away from their faces.

"Yes, those are Briggs and Drake," Clint said. "How'd they get here?"

"The sheriff brought them."

"That clinches it, then," Clint said. "Whatever's going on, the sheriff's in on it."

"Over here."

Jeffrey took Clint to the feed bin and opened it.

"That your clerk?"

"That's him," Clint said, and Jeffrey dropped the lid. "You didn't find another woman's body, did you?"

"No," Jeffrey said, "but I stopped looking after I found the clerk."

"Let's look around, then," Clint said. "Maybe she's in here."

They stayed together because of the one lamp, but didn't find any more bodies.

"Let's get out of this stink," Clint said.

They went out the back door.

"What are you gonna do about the sheriff?"

"Who do we report him to?" Clint asked. "There's no other law."

"Take care of him yourself, then," Jeffrey said.

"I might have to."

"Especially after I tell you what else I found out."

"About the sheriff?"

Jeffrey nodded.

"Well, spit it out."

"Maybe we can renegotiate my pay?" Jeffrey asked.

"We might," Clint said, "After I hear what you have to say."

"The sheriff's been reporting to someone here in town," Jeffrey said.

"Who?"

"I'm gettin' to that," the man said. "He's a pretty powerful man around here."

"Rich?"

"Very."

"I don't know who I hate more," Clint said, "rich men, or politicians."

"This one," Jeffrey said, "is both."

Chapter Twenty-Nine

"Okay, that needs explaining."

"Split Rail has a resident who spends time here, and in Washington," Jeffrey said.

"Why?" Clint asked. "What's here that's not in Washington, for a politician?"

"He has a ranch near here," Jeffrey said. "When he started running for public office, he got himself a small office in town so he could be close to the telegraph line."

"And this is the man Patterson is reporting to?"

"That's him."

"Okay, Jeffrey," Clint said. "What's his name?"

"William Demarest Maxwell," Jeffrey said. "Representative Maxwell."

Clint hesitated, then said, "You're kidding. Split Rail has a politician in residence? Wyoming's not even a state."

"It's provisional," Jeffrey said. "When Wyoming does become a state, he'll run as a—what do they call it—grass . . . ?"

"Grass roots candidate?"

"That's it," Jeffrey said. "He promised people he'd never be far from his home, in Wyoming."

Clint fell silent.

"Are you wonderin' what a Representative is doin' mixed up with murder?"

"No," Clint said, with a snort. "Politicians deal in murder all the time. No, I'm wondering what's going on in Split Rail that rates killing three people, and making Angela Brown disappear?"

"So what are you gonna do?"

"I figure the best way to get answers to those questions," Clint said, "is to ask him."

***

Clint found out from Jeffrey where the Representative's office was, and his ranch. He decided to try the office first. He'd prefer to find him there than out at his ranch, with his crew behind him.

"Want me to go with you?" Jeffrey asked.

Clint handed him some money.

"No, you did what I wanted you to do," Clint said. "You're done."

"This is more than we agreed on," Jeffrey said.

"You earned it," Clint assured him.

He didn't want Jeffrey to go with him, but then he got an idea.

***

As he entered the sheriff's office, the man looked up from the coffee cup he was filling at the potbellied stove.

"Mr. Adams," Patterson said, "just the man I wanted to see." He put the pot down and walked to his desk without offering Clint a cup.

"What's on your mind, sheriff?"

"I'm afraid the people you've been lookin' for have all just . . . vanished. I can't find any sign of them. I'm sorry."

"I appreciate the effort, sheriff," Clint said. "Perhaps there's one more thing I can ask you to do for me, and then maybe I'll just have to move on."

"Well," Patterson said, that news seeming to boost him, "what is it?"

"Take me to see the Representative."

Patterson was in the act of sipping his coffee and almost choked.

"The Representative?"

"Yes," Clint said, "isn't that what they call him, Representative Maxwell?"

"Why would you wanna see him?" Patterson asked. "He's a pretty busy man."

"Seems to me he'd be concerned that some of his constituents have disappeared . . . or worse."

"Well, yeah, of course—"

"And I think it would be better for you to take me to see him than for me to just go in without warning."

"I suppose I could—"

"Is he in town, or at his ranch now?"

"You know about his ranch?"

"Hey," Clint said, "it isn't every town that has a Representative living in it."

"No, I guess not," Patterson said. "Suppose I have a word with Maxwell and . . . set it up?"

"That'd be great," Clint said. "I'll be at my hotel when you're ready."

"Uh, sure," Patterson said. "I'll come by to fetch you."

"Thanks, Sheriff," Clint said. "You've been very helpful since I got to Split Rail."

"I'm . . . just doin' my job, Mr. Adams," Patterson said.

"And it's a fine job you're doing, too," Clint told the man. "I'll see you later."

Clint left the office and with a big grin, started for his hotel.

Chapter Thirty

Clint went back to his hotel, which he was sick of already. In fact, he was sick of Split Rail, Wyoming, and hoped that meeting with Representative Maxwell was going to be the last piece in the puzzle of Angela Brown and her disappearance.

***

"He wants to what?" Representative William Demarest Maxwell demanded.

"He wants to meet you, and talk to you," Sheriff Patterson said.

"Why?" Maxwell asked, sitting back in his chair. "Who gave him my name?"

"I have no idea, sir," Patterson said. "It wasn't me. He just hit me with it out of the blue."

Maxwell turned his chair around and stared out the window.

"Why should I?" he finally said. "Why should I agree?"

"Well," the sheriff said "if I could answer that question . . ."

Maxwell turned back around and stared at Patterson.

"Go ahead," he said.

"We gotta remember who we're dealin' with," the lawman said. "This is the Gunsmith. If you refuse to see him, it's gonna make him want it even more. And he'll come for you."

Maxwell rubbed his jaw and gave the matter some thought.

"All right," he said, finally, "Bring him to the ranch tomorrow morning. I'll have a bunch of men around me, then."

"There's a man in town whose gun might just be able to go up against Adams."

"Who's that?"

"His name's Frank Jeffrey."

"Get him out here, then," Maxwell said. "Maybe we can push Adams into a fight and get rid of him, instead of worrying about him."

"I'll see what I can do."

"Don't see if you can," Maxwell said, "just get him."

"It's short notice."

"Okay, then," Maxwell said, "bring Adams out in the afternoon. That'll give you a few more hours."

"You'll have to pay him, you know," Patterson said. "Jeffrey, I mean. His gun's for hire."

"Fine," Maxwell said. "That's probably what I should've done from the beginning. In fact, I probably should've had her . . ." He trailed off.

"Have who do what?" Patterson asked.

"Never mind," Maxwell said standing. "I better ride out to the ranch and get a reception ready for Mr. Adams."

"Without Jeffrey?"

"I'll make plans so I can slot him in," Maxwell said. "Just make sure he knows what's going to be expected of him."

"Going up against the Gunsmith," Patterson said. "You might not even have to pay him for that."

"And make sure he knows he's going to get paid."

"Yes, sir."

They left the office together, Maxwell locking up behind them.

"Get going," he told the lawman. "I don't want us seen together on the street."

"Yes, sir."

Patterson crossed over to the other side of the street and then started back toward the center of town. Maxwell waited a few more minutes, then headed for a nearby livery where he kept his horse and his buggy. He got the animal hitched up, and headed for his ranch.

***

The woman looked out the window of her second floor room and saw William Maxwell pull up in his buggy. He got out, handed it off to one of his men, and then hurried toward the house. She turned, left her room to rush downstairs to catch him.

As she got to the bottom of the stairs, the front door opened and Maxwell came in.

"Simms!" He shouted for his man.

"William," she said, "how much longer?"

"One moment, my dear," Maxwell said.

A tall, whited-haired man in a cream colored suit came rushing into the front hall.

"Sir?"

"Find Hutch and bring him here right away."

"Yes, sir."

Simms left the house to go and find Dan Hutchinson, the foreman of the ranch.

He looked at the woman and said, "Let's go upstairs."

"Why are you sending for Hutch?"

"We're going to have a visitor tomorrow, and I want to get things ready."

"Ready for who?" Angela Brown asked.

"Your friend," he said, "Clint Adams."

He took her elbow and led her up the stairs.

Chapter Thirty-One

Even with the short notice, it didn't take Sheriff Patterson long to locate Frank Jeffrey at the Riverboat Saloon. The gunman was sitting alone at a table with a half-finished beer.

Patterson went to the bar, got two fresh beers and carried them over to the table.

"Mind if I sit?"

Jeffrey looked up, seemed surprised to find the lawman standing there.

"You're the law," Jeffrey said.

Patterson sat and pushed one of the beers over to Jeffrey. The gunman drained the one he had and closed his hand around the fresh one.

"What do I owe you for this?" he asked.

"A job," the sheriff said. "Just a job."

"For you?" Jeffrey asked, surprised.

"For the Representative."

That surprised Jeffrey even more . . .

***

When Jeffrey first saw the lawman enter the saloon he figured he'd just ignore him. But when the man came over to his table carrying two beers, he wondered if he had spotted him following him earlier?

But when the sheriff mentioned the Representative, Jeffrey was really surprised . . . and curious . . .

***

"What's the job?" Jeffrey asked.

"The Representative needs you to handle somebody for him," the lawman said.

"When?"

"Tomorrow afternoon, out at his ranch."

"Does he know I ain't cheap?"

"He knows," the sheriff said.

"Who's the job?"

"I think you're gonna like this," Sheriff Patterson said. "It's Clint Adams, the Gunsmith."

"That *is* interesting," Jeffrey admitted. "What's he *want* me to do?"

"Well," Patterson said, "if it comes to it, he wants you to kill 'im."

Jeffrey sat back, cradling his fresh beer.

"When does he want me?"

"I'll be bringing Adams out to his ranch in the afternoon," Patterson said, "so you better get there in the mornin' so the Representative can tell you what he's plannin'."

Jeffrey nodded and said, "Yeah, okay, I can do that."

"Can you take the Gunsmith, Jeffrey?"

"Sure I can."

"What makes you so sure?" the lawman asked.

"He ain't as young as he used to be, is he?" Jeffrey asked. "Which probably means he ain't as fast."

Patterson hadn't touched his beer, so he pushed it over to Jeffrey and stood up.

"Then I'll see you out at the ranch," he said. "If we come face-to-face—"

"Don't worry," Jeffrey said. "I ain't seen you, lately."

"Right."

The lawman turned and walked out of the Riverboat, wondering if Frank Jeffrey was as good as he thought he was?

***

Jeffrey worked on the first beer, figuring to finish it before the second one got too warm. He'd never before been hired to kill a man he had just finished working for.

Of course, his pay day from the Representative was going to be much bigger than what he got from the

131

Gunsmith—and he didn't really owe Adams anything. After all, a job was a job.

And the long range benefits of killing the Gunsmith were limitless.

He finished the first beer the sheriff had given him, and grabbed the second.

***

Sheriff Patterson went straight to the livery stable from the Riverboat Saloon to saddle his horse. He needed to ride out to the Representative's ranch to let the man know that Frank Jeffrey had agreed to the job. He hated the thought of going out there, because it would be dark by the time he got back, but Representative Maxwell would insist on knowing ahead of time that his pieces were in place. And Patterson knew the way there and back well enough to ride it in the dark.

***

When Maxwell and Angela Brown got to the second floor, the Representative led her to his bedroom, and closed the door behind them.

"What's going on?" she demanded.

The Representative started to undress, speaking as he did.

"The sheriff is bringing Clint Adams out here tomorrow afternoon," he said. "I'm going to have him taken care of."

"Is that really necessary?"

"If you hadn't spent time with him, and been seen doing it, killing three people wouldn't have been necessary. When I hire you to do a job, I expect you to lay low until it's time to do it."

"So I got hungry," she said.

"And was seen in public with him?" Maxwell snapped. "And went back to his room with him?"

"I had . . . urges," she said, weakly.

"Well, I have them, too," he said. "Get undressed."

"Representative—"

Maxwell pointed a finger at her, standing there bare-chested.

"You messed this up for me," he snapped. "All you had to do was stay out of sight until I needed you."

"Representative—"

"Do you want your fee?"

"Of course I do—"

"Then get those clothes off and do what you're supposed to do."

She stared at him while he pulled off his boots and trousers and sat on the bed, naked, waiting, a vicious grin on his face.

With great reluctance she undressed and, when she was fully naked, walked to the bed. She stood in front of him, tall and proud with seemingly acres of delicious flesh on display. But as he reached for her, she suddenly slapped his face.

"Get on your back!" she ordered.

"Yes, mistress," he said.

Obediently, he fell onto his back. She decided not to go to his closet, where there was an assortment of whips and chains they had used before. Instead, she got to her knees, slid her hands over his pale thighs, and then dug her nails into them. Rather than groan in pain, William Maxwell moaned out loud in pleasure.

Angela moved her hands to his half erect cock and began to stroke it with one hand, while squeezing his testicles with the other. This time the sounds he emitted were a mixture of pleasure and pain. Angela's only salvation here was that she knew Maxwell would not last very long under her expert ministrations. In fact, when she lowered her head, engulfed his cock, taking it fully into her mouth, it only took a few bobs of her head for him to cry out loudly, and explode . . .

Chapter Thirty-Two

When the knock came at the door, Angela groaned, but Maxwell came awake.

"What is it?" he demanded.

"I'm sorry, sir," Simms said through the door, "but the sheriff is downstairs."

"All right," Maxwell said, "I'll be there in a minute."

He sat up in bed, looked down at the scratches on his thighs, started to touch them, but then pulled his hand away because of the pain. Angela remained on her stomach, asleep. He stood up, got dressed and left the room.

Seconds after he had gone, Angela rolled out of bed, and dressed quickly. When he came back, she wanted to be in her own room, and hopefully he wouldn't come to get her.

***

Downstairs Maxwell found Sheriff Patterson waiting at the foot of the steps.

"Sorry to disturb you sir," Patterson said, quickly, "but you wanted to know when I got Frank Jeffrey to agree—"

"Yes, yes," Maxwell said, "get to it."

Patterson would have liked to be offered a refreshment of some kind after his ride, but knew it wasn't to be.

"Okay, well, Jeffrey agreed, and he'll ride out here tomorrow mornin' so you can tell him what you want, and where you want him."

"Good."

"And then I'll bring Adams out in the afternoon."

"Fine. Then I want you to leave."

"Don't you think you'll need—"

"I don't need that badge anywhere near here," Maxwell said. "Especially when I'm not sure exactly what's going to transpire."

"Okay," Patterson said, "you're the boss."

"Just remember that at all times," Maxwell said, "and we'll be fine."

"Yes, sir."

"Now get back to town."

Patterson nodded, turned and left the house, Simms closing the door firmly behind him.

Simms looked over at Maxwell, who was wearing his white shirt with most of the buttons undone, trousers, but not his boots.

"Sir," he asked, "will you be going back up, or . . ."

"Not just yet, Simms," the Representative said. "I'm going to have a brandy. Would you please tell cook to put something out in the diningroom for me to eat?"

"Yes, sir."

As Simms went to the kitchen, Maxwell looked down at himself, saw a scratch on his chest that had left some blood on his shirt. He wondered if Patterson had noticed it?

Buttoning his shirt, he started walking to his office, where he kept the good brandy.

Chapter Thirty-Three

Clint had breakfast in the morning at his hotel, not wanting to miss Sheriff Patterson if the man came to fetch him early. As it turned out, he remained in his room until it was afternoon. He was reading when the knock came on his door. He had his holster around his waist, so he simply stood and walked to the door.

"Sheriff?"

"Who else would it be?"

He opened the door.

"You ready to go?" Patterson asked. He seemed nervous.

"Are you all right?" Clint asked.

"I'm fine," Patterson said. "I've just got things to do, so I'll take you out to the Representative's, and then head back."

"That's fine with me," Clint said. "All I need is the introduction."

As they started walking downstairs, Patterson said, "I have to warn you, the Representative is not an easy man to talk to."

"Politicians rarely are," Clint said.

***

When Angela came down for breakfast, Representative Maxwell was already eating.

"You didn't come to my room last night," she said, sitting across from him.

"When I got back you were gone, I assumed you were . . . tired," Maxwell said.

The cook, a middle-aged woman with black hair shot with grey, came out of the kitchen and set a plate down in front of Angela.

"Thank you, Lily."

The cook simply nodded, turned and left. Angela poured herself a cup of coffee from the pot on the table.

"When will Adams be getting here?" she asked.

"Sometime after noon," Maxwell said.

"And where do you want me?"

"In your room, unless I send for you," the Representative answered.

"And under what circumstance would you do that?"

"We might have to satisfy the Gunsmith that Angela Brown is alive and well," he said.

"Or?" she asked.

"Or I might need you in a more professional capacity."

"Well then," she said, "I better be ready for either."

"Indeed," Maxwell said.

***

When Clint rode up to the ranch house with Sheriff Patterson, it drew the attention of half a dozen or so ranch hands who were milling about or working. The setup was impressive, with a two story house, a huge barn and corral, and a large bunkhouse. In the corral were a good-looking group of horses.

They reined in their horses in front of the house, and a tall man approached them. He was Dan Hutchinson, the foreman of the ranch, and he had orders from the Representative to make the two men feel welcome—initially.

"Been expectin' you gents," he said. "I can have your horses cared for."

He started to wave to someone, but Clint said, "That's okay. I don't think I'll be here that long, and the sheriff needs to return to town."

"That's right," Patterson said. "I only had to bring him here, Hutch. I gotta get back."

"Well, okay, then, Sheriff," Hutch said "Good seein' ya."

Patterson looked at Clint.

"I hope this works out for you."

"Yeah, thanks," Clint said, aware that the man was lying through his teeth.

Patterson turned his horse and headed back to town.

"If you want to dismount, Mr. Adams," Hutchinson said, "I'll take you to the Representative."

Clint stepped down from the saddle.

"I'm Dan Hutchinson, the foreman," the man said, sticking out his hand.

Clint shook it shortly, not wanting his gun hand to be occupied for very long.

"Quite an operation," he commented.

"Yeah, the Representative keeps us on our toes. He likes to know things are goin' smoothly whenever he has to leave and go to Washington."

"And how often is that?"

"Oh, 'bout half the time, I reckon."

"And he leaves you in charge of everything?" Clint asked.

"Everythin' but the house," Hutchinson said. "That job belongs to Simms. You'll meet him as soon as you go through the front door."

"Might as well not waste any more time then," Clint commented.

Hutchinson waved his hand and said, "After you."

Chapter Thirty-Four

As they went through the front door Clint saw a tall white-haired man waiting just inside, his hands clasped behind his back.

"Mr. Hutchinson," he said.

"Simms, this is Mr. Clint Adams," the foreman said, "the man the boss is waitin' for." Hutchinson looked at Clint. "I'll leave you in Simms' hands now."

"Thank you."

The foreman nodded and went out the front door.

"May I take your gun, sir?" Simms asked.

"No, you may not, Simms."

"I'd really rather you don't see the Representative while armed, sir," the man said.

Clint studied the man, didn't see any lumps under his coat that would indicate he was armed, so he was making this request with only the backing of his words.

"Mr. Simms—" Clint started.

"Just Simms, sir."

"Simms," Clint said, "I don't go anywhere without this gun and this gun doesn't go anywhere without me. Is that clear enough?"

"It's what the Representative told me you'd say, sir. I just had to try to do my job."

"Are you the Representative's bodyguard, then?"

"Among other things," Simms said. "If you'll follow me, I'll take you to him."

"Lead on, Simms."

Clint had been in rich men's homes before. He was either being led to a plushly furnished living room, or a rich man's den or library. When they passed the living room—furnished as he had imagined—he knew it was the latter.

He followed Simms down a hall and entered a room he had never seen the likes of before, but nevertheless was familiar with. The walls were lined with books, and there was a desk in front of a window. Behind the desk was a 50ish, dark-haired, soft looking man he assumed was Representative William Maxwell.

"Sir, Mr. Adams is here," Simms said. "He would not give up his weapon."

"And I didn't expect him to," Maxwell said. "Mr. Adams, please, have a seat."

The man stood and gave Clint a politician's smile, but did not come out from behind the desk. Instead, he extended his hand across it.

Clint approached the desk and shook the man's hand shortly. He was sure a man like the Representative would have a gun in one of his desk drawers.

He took the man's invitation and sat across from him, as the Representative seated himself.

"That'll be all, Simms," he said to his man.

"Sir, as I said, he would not give up his gun—"

"He's not going to shoot me, Simms," Maxwell said, then looked at Clint and added, "Are you?"

"It's not my intention," Clint said.

"See? Now go!"

Simms left.

"Now," the Representative said, "the sheriff tells me you want to talk to me about something."

"Have you ever met a woman named Angela Brown?" Clint asked.

"Angela Brown," Maxwell said thinking. "If she voted for me, I'd probably remember, but . . . no, I don't think I have."

"You have three voters in Split Rail who have . . . disappeared," Clint said. "They may even be dead."

"That's horrible."

Clint decided to change tactics.

"What's your ultimate goal, Mr. Representative?"

"My goal?"

"Yes," Clint said. "How high do you think you can go? Senator? President?"

"Hey, who knows?" Maxwell asked. "I'm just trying to do the best for my people. When Wyoming becomes a state, I want to be able to make a difference."

"For your people? In Split Rail."

"The people of Wyoming," the Representative said. "That's who I represent."

"Well, three of your people are dead."

Maxell pointed a finger at Clint.

"You said they were missing and might be dead."

"Oh, they're dead."

"And how do you know that?"

"Because I found their bodies," Clint said.

"You . . . you found them?" Maxwell asked. "I'm confused. Why didn't you say that in the first place?"

"I was trying to figure out if you knew."

"How would I know?" Maxwell asked. "Have you told the sheriff about these bodies?"

"No."

"Why not?"

"Because I think he killed them," Clint said. "At the very least, he's the one who hid the bodies."

Maxwell stared a few moments, then asked, "Are you serious?"

"Furthermore," Clint said, "I think you know as much as he does."

"How's that?"

"He's been reporting to you," Clint said. "Every move he makes, every move I make."

"And how do you know that?"

"Because I had him followed."

Maxwell stared again, this time longer.

"Yeah, that's right," Clint said. "I know that you and the sheriff are behind the murders. What I don't know is why. You want to tell me that?"

Maxwell remained silent.

"And I'm going to need you to tell me what happened to Angela Brown," Clint said. "Is she dead, too? Because I haven't found her body. . . yet."

"Angela Brown," Maxwell said, then. "There is no Angela Brown, Mr. Adams. There never was."

"That's what you wanted me to believe," Clint said. "That's why you got rid of anyone who saw her with me. But I saw her. I was with her. I know she exists."

"The woman you were with exists," Maxwell said, "that's true. What I'm telling you is . . . her name is not Angela Brown. And it never was."

Chapter Thirty-Five

"I think you're going to have to explain that," Clint said.

Maxwell stood up.

"If you'll wait here, I'll have her explain it herself," he said.

"She's here?" Clint asked.

"Yes, and she's very much alive," Maxwell said. "I'll— just be a moment."

The Representative came around the desk and left the room. Clint walked to the sidebar and helped himself to what he was sure was expensive brandy—not because he liked it, but because he felt it would bother Maxwell when he came back.

***

Maxwell found Simms waiting in the entry hall.

"Sir?"

"I'm going upstairs to bring the lady down," he told his man. "When I come back, I want Frank Jeffrey to be here."

"Yes, sir."

The Representative went up the stairs, down the hall to "Angela Brown's" room. He knew he could have just walked in, but instead he knocked on the closed door.

"Representative," she said, when she opened it. "How's it going?"

"Your friend would like to see you," Maxwell said. "Please come downstairs with me."

"Shall I bring . . . anything?" she asked.

"I just want you to talk to him," the Representative said. "Assure him that you're fine. Oh, and possibly tell him your real name."

"And why I was in town?"

Maxwell hesitated, then said, "Not exactly."

"Well, what then?"

"Go and put your boots on," he said, "and then I'll tell you exactly what I want you to tell him."

***

While the Representative was away, Clint took the opportunity to go through the man's desk. As he had suspected, he found a .32 Colt in the top drawer. He took the time to unload it and pocket the shells, then picked his brandy snifter up from the desk and returned to his chair.

***

As Maxwell came down the stairs with Angela, Frank Jeffrey watched from the bottom.

"Are you gonna introduce me—" he started to say, giving Angela an admiring look.

"Not the time, Jeffrey, and not what you're here for. Adams is in my office. I want you out in the hall, and if I call—"

"—I kill him?"

"Precisely. Follow me."

He took Angela's arm again, led her down the hall with Jeffrey behind them.

When Maxwell reentered the office with Angela Brown, Clint stood up, brandishing his brandy snifter. Watching Maxwell's reaction, he was satisfied to see that the man indeed wasn't pleased. As Maxwell went back behind his desk Clint turned his attention to Angela.

"Are you all right?" he asked her.

"I'm fine, Clint."

"I've been worried sick," he said. "So many people have been trying to convince me that you don't exist."

"Well, here I am."

"But your name isn't Angela Brown?"

"No, it's not."

"I think I'm going to need a little more than that."

Maxwell said, "I'm going to let you two talk," and left the office.

***

Representative Maxwell stepped out into the hall and as Frank Jeffrey started to speak to him, he held a finger to his pursed lips, then cupped a hand to his ear.

They both listened.

Chapter Thirty-Six

"You want a glass of the Representative's excellent brandy?" Clint asked her.

"Sure, why not?" she said. After all, the Representative himself had never offered her any.

Clint poured and handed her a snifter. He put his down on the desk, then sat in the Representative's chair. Why not just go ahead and annoy the man as much as he could? Besides, he had a clear view of the door from there, and he sat so that the thick back of the chair was between him and the window.

"Why don't you tell me what's going on, Ang—or whatever your name is."

"My name is Helena Briscoe," she said.

"Why the lie?"

"Because, like I told you, I was here to do a job. The job was—is—for the Representative, but he didn't want anyone to know I was in town. But I got hungry, and decided to go out and get something to eat. You know the rest."

"So you became 'Angela Brown' just so you could have something to eat."

"Yes," she said, "and when it went further between us . . . well, I was stuck with that name."

"Okay," he said, "now tell me why everyone who saw you with me had to die."

"What?" She looked confused. "I don't know anything about anyone dying."

"Is that a fact?"

"Yes, it is," she said. "Believe me, nobody's spoken to me about it."

"Not even the Representative?"

She sniffed rudely and said, "He never would."

"And what's this job you're supposed to do for him?" Clint asked.

"You're going to have to ask him," she said. "I can't say."

"Angel—Helena," Clint said. "three people have been killed because they saw you with me. They tried to convince me that you didn't exist, and they failed."

"And who do you think did it?"

"I think it was done by the Representative's order," Clint said.

"Why would he do such a thing?"

"To hide the fact that you were here."

"That sounds awfully drastic, Clint," she said. "What do you think you can do about it?"

"Nothing," he said.

"Nothing?"

"Murder's the sheriff's business," he said. "My goal was to find you and make sure you were safe. Obviously, you are. If you don't want to tell me what your business with the Representative is, that's up to you. But now that I'm satisfied you're all right—and weren't a figment of my imagination—I'll be on my way."

"I'm sorry we didn't get to spend more time together," she said.

"So am I." He stood up. "I suppose I should tell the Representative I'm going."

At that point, as if on cue, the man appeared in the doorway.

***

In the hall, listening intently to the conversation, the Representative then leaned over to Jeffrey.

"You can go," he said, in a low whisper.

"Why? You don't want him killed?"

"You heard him," Maxwell said. "He's leaving town."

"And you believe him?"

Maxwell made a chopping gesture with his hand, to cut Jeffrey off from any further objection.

"Stay around, then," he said. "We'll talk later. But now . . . go!"

Reluctantly, Jeffrey turned and walked up the hall.

When Clint Adams said, "I suppose I should tell the Representative I'm going," Maxwell chose that moment to reenter the room.

***

"I hope you don't mind me sitting in your chair and drinking your brandy," Clint said, as he came out from behind the desk.

"Actually, I do," Maxwell said, "but what's done is done." He walked around and took his chair. "Are you satisfied?"

"That Angel—Helena is all right? Yes. She says she has a job to do for you, but won't tell me what it is."

"That's not your business."

"I still think three people have been killed because they saw her," Clint said.

"And you think I had something to do with that?"

"You know what?" Clint answered. "I don't care. None of this is my business. As long as she's all right, I'll be leaving town."

"That's good news," Maxwell said. "When?"

"Tomorrow," he said. "I'd leave from here, but I need to collect some things from my room."

"I'll have Simms show you to the door, then."

"I can find my way to the door." Clint turned to Angela/Helena. "Good-bye."

"Good-bye, Clint. And . . . thanks for being worried about me."

Clint left without another word to the Representative.

***

After Clint Adams left the house, Simms came in.

"Is he gone?" the Representative asked.

"Yes, sir. Out the door and on his horse."

"Good. Now go and find Frank Jeffrey and bring him in here."

"Yes, sir."

"Who's he?" Helena asked.

"Never mind. Once we know Adams has left town tomorrow, I'm going to want you to do what I'm paying you to do. For now, you can go back to your room."

"I'm going to sleep," she said. "Don't wake me."

She left the office, and as she walked back up the hall, a man was coming the other way.

"Frank Jeffrey?" she asked.

"That's right."

"He's waiting for you."

"Too bad," Jeffrey said. "Maybe you and I can meet later?"

"I'm going to bed," she said.

"Good," he said, with a smile. "Wait for me there."

"You can come up if you want," she told him, "but I sleep with a knife, and I'm not afraid to use it."

He laughed and continued on to the office.

Chapter Thirty-Seven

"Close the door," Maxwell said.

Jeffrey did so, then turned.

"Who was the girl?" he asked.

"Never mind," the Representative said, "Have a seat."

"Is Adams gone?"

"Yes, he's on his way back to town."

Jeffrey sat.

"I don't understand," he said. "I thought you wanted me to kill him."

"If necessary," Maxwell said, "and it still might be."

"How will I know?"

"I'll tell you," Maxwell said. "He says he's leaving town tomorrow. He says certain things that have happened in town aren't his business."

"Things like . . .?"

"Never mind," Maxwell said. "Let's just say I'm not sure I believe him."

"So what do you want me to do?"

"If he leaves as he says he's going to, nothing," the Representative said.

"And if he doesn't?"

Maxwell sat forward in his chair.

"Then kill him."

Jeffrey sat back in his.

"Let's discuss my fee."

***

Clint rode back to town, on the alert for a possible ambush. He wasn't all that sure the Representative believed what he said about leaving town. He wasn't even sure he believed it. Would he be able to pack up and ride out, leaving three dead people behind him? Why was it his responsibility to do anything? Angela turned out to be Helena, and a liar. The best thing for him to do would be to pack up and head out.

But the thing that kept bringing him back was Patterson, the crooked sheriff. He hated bent lawmen. He'd worn a badge long enough himself, early in his career, to know that he never wanted to wear one again, but he still respected what it represented. And seeing Patterson wearing a badge irked him.

By the time he got back to town he figured he better make it look like he was leaving town, and then double back. The thing to do was probably return to that barn and move those bodies, so the sheriff couldn't dispose of them. Or maybe just confront the man head on and make him take off the badge.

He directed Eclipse back to the livery stable. He still had tonight to do something—or to have something done to him.

***

Frank Jeffrey rode into Split Rail about an hour after Clint returned. His pockets were bulging with Representative Maxwell's money. And since he had been paid in advance for a job, he was going to have to do it.

He actually liked Clint Adams, but that didn't mean he wouldn't kill him.

***

The only way to move those bodies was with a buckboard. The hostler was so happy to have Eclipse back in his barn, that he agreed to rent Clint a buckboard and two horses, cheap.

"Whataya gonna use 'em for?" the man asked.

"Hauling," Clint said, and left it at that.

By the time he drove the buckboard from the livery to the dilapidated barn, it was dark, which was good. He left the buckboard just outside the back door, and carried the bodies one-by-one out to it. Once he had them loaded, he just stood there, staring at them, wondering what the hell he was going to do with them now?

Chapter Thirty-Eight

When he finally decided where to take them, he drove the buckboard there—carefully, in the dark. He didn't want to bring the horses back to the livery lame from stepping in a chuckhole.

The only place he could think of to take the bodies was right back to where he first saw two of them—Drake's shack.

He stopped in front of the shack, went inside, found a lamp and lit it, then brought the bodies inside. He hoped when the sheriff discovered they were gone, he wouldn't think to look back there.

He blew the lamp out and drove the buckboard back to the livery, which was closed at that time. He unhitched the team, put them back in the corral behind the barn, and left the buckboard for the hostler to find when he came back in the morning to open up.

All of that done, he returned to his hotel, still being very alert for an attempt on his life. But while there were no shots coming, he did encounter a man with a gun in the lobby of the hotel.

"I thought our business was done," he said to Frank Jeffrey.

"Ours is, yeah," Jeffrey said, "but now I've been hired by somebody else."

Clint got it, immediately.

"Don't tell me, let me guess—the Representative?"

"You got it the first time."

"So what's the job?" Clint asked. "Kill me right here in the lobby?"

"Naw," Jeffrey said, "he just wants to make sure you really are leavin' in the mornin'."

"So you're my escort?"

"Let's just say I'm gonna be around to watch and make sure."

"And if I don't leave?"

"Then things could get ugly."

"Well," Clint said, "I guess we'll just have to wait until morning to find out."

"I guess so," Jeffrey said. "I'll see you then."

Clint waited until Jeffrey actually left the building before turning and heading for the stairs. He noticed the hotel manager, Feeny, was at the desk.

"Say hello to your wife for me," he said, as he passed, leaving the man looking puzzled.

***

162

In the morning, Clint used the time spent at breakfast to go over the events of the night before—his conversations with the Representative and Angela/Helena, moving the bodies, and then his exchange with Frank Jeffrey down in the hotel lobby. He was still torn between leaving town, and staying to get justice for the three dead people—especially that poor waitress, Nancy, who had done nothing wrong.

And then there was Sheriff Patterson and his badge. He wanted to tear it off the man's chest, but now it seemed before he could do that, he was going to have to deal with Frank Jeffrey.

Maybe . . .

***

Clint decided to mount up and ride out of town. When he was far enough out as not to be seen, he'd turn around and ride back in.

He checked out of the hotel under the baleful stare of the manager, Feeny, then stepped outside. He looked up and down the street, then at the other side. There was no sign of Jeffrey, but the man had already demonstrated that he could go unseen when he wanted to. But if Jeffrey was telling the truth, he wouldn't make a try at Clint as long as it looked like he was riding out.

He walked to the livery and told the hostler he wanted Eclipse.

"Goin' for anther ride?" the man asked.

"Leaving town," Clint said.

"For good?"

"Yes," Clint said, "so I'll also want to settle my bill."

"Hey," the man said, "I should be payin' you for puttin' an animal like that in my shop. Uh, but that don't mean—"

"Don't worry," Clint said. "I'll pay."

"I'll saddle 'im," the man said. "It'll gimme a chance to say goodbye."

"Go ahead, if he'll let you," Clint said, handing the man his saddlebags.

"Oh, he'll let me," the man said. "Me and him have come to an understandin'."

"That's good to hear," Clint said, absently.

"It won't take long."

As the hostler went to take care of saddling Eclipse, Clint walked to the doors and looked outside. Still no sign of Jeffrey, or the sheriff. It looked, for all intents and purposes, like no one was interested in him.

If that were only true.

Chapter Thirty-Nine

Clint found a back way into town that put him behind the buildings on the main street—which included the sheriff's office. His intention was to grab the sheriff and walk him over to Drake's shack, where he had put the bodies. Once there, they'd have a conversation about who killed who.

He stopped directly behind the jail and dismounted. The old building had a back door which led directly to the cell block, as most old jailhouses did. He tried the door, found it locked, but flimsy. A good push with his shoulder against it, and the door popped open.

He stepped inside as quietly as he could, saw that there were two empty cells. Beyond them was the doorway that led to the office. He stayed still and listened, didn't hear anything at first, but then someone took a deep breath and let it out, then the shuffling of some papers. Somebody was in the office, and since there were no deputies, it was likely to be Sheriff Patterson.

He moved past the cells to the doorway and peered into the next room. Sure enough, Patterson was sitting at his desk, shuffling papers. Was he trying to look busy, in case anyone peered in the window?

Clint stepped in and said, "Just sit still, Sheriff."

Patterson froze.

"That you, Adams?"

"It's me."

"I thought you left town."

"That's what you were supposed to think," Clint said. "Where's your gun?"

"Hanging on the wall peg."

"Good. Now you're going to get up slowly, and we're going out the back door. I want to see your open hands the whole time."

Patterson stood, his hands up and open.

"Where are we headed?"

"You'll see," Clint said. "Just walk to me, and then to the back door."

Patterson walked, looking nervous.

"You wouldn't be takin' me somewhere quiet just to shoot me, would ya?"

"I don't make a habit of shooting men who wear badges," Clint said. "Let's just say we're going somewhere quiet to have a little talk."

"No—why not—"

"And no more talk until we get there," Clint snapped.

***

Clint walked Patterson out of town toward Drake's shack, with Eclipse walking behind him.

"Oh, I get it," Patterson said, halfway there, "but why are we goin'—"

"No talking until we get there," Clint said.

The lawman shrugged and fell silent.

When they reached the shack Clint told eclipse to stay, and walked Patterson inside. The man immediately caught the smell, then saw the blanket wrapped bodies.

"What the—" he started.

"That's right, Sheriff," Clint said. "You moved them from here to that barn, and I moved them back. Have a seat."

Patterson sat in a rickety wooden chair and tried not to look at the blankets.

"I don't understand," he said. "Whose bodies—"

"Let's not play that game, Sheriff," Clint said. "Let's just start with the knowledge that we both know whose bodies these are."

"I don't—"

"Or maybe you're right," Clint said. "Maybe I should just shoot you."

"Okay, now wait," Patterson said. "Okay, yeah, I know whose bodies those are."

"Good, now we're getting somewhere. You just need to admit you killed them."

"What? Naw, are you crazy—"

"If you're not going to cooperate—"

"You can shoot me if you wanna," Patterson said, loudly, "but I ain't gonna admit I killed 'em, because I didn't. Okay, I moved the bodies, but that's it."

"Why'd you move them?"

Patterson fell silent.

"For Representative Maxwell? Did he tell you to hide them?" Clint asked. "So that I wouldn't know they were dead, I'd just think they were gone?"

"You seem to know a lot," Patterson said.

"I figured out a lot," Clint said. "All I need is for you to confirm it."

"And then what?"

"And then I'm going to have to get a federal marshal in here to make some arrests," Clint said, "because you won't be wearing that badge, anymore."

Chapter Forty

"The Representative brought Helena in for a job he wanted her to do, but didn't want anyone to know who she was. So when she was seen with me, he had to get rid of the people who saw her. And try to convince me she never existed."

"Keep goin'," Patterson said. "You ain't gonna believe this, but some of this I don't even know."

"This is the part I don't understand," Clint said. "Why kill them and not me? I mean, I actually spent time with the woman."

"Killin' you woulda brought Split Rail too much attention," Patterson said.

"I can see that, but he thought when everybody disappeared, I'd just leave town?"

Patterson shrugged.

"I guess he was hopin'."

"So he had a desk clerk, a waitress and a café owner killed," Clint said. "And you're saying you didn't do it?"

"That's right," Patterson said. "I didn't. I do lots of jobs for the Representative, but I don't kill people."

"Then who did?"

"I don't know."

"Well, it's either your job to hide the bodies for Maxwell," Clint said, "or to find out who killed them. Which is it?"

"If you'd ever worn a badge—" Patterson said.

"I did," Clint said, cutting him off. "Years ago. And I gave it up, because it was never appreciated. At least not in the towns where I wore it."

"Then you know," Patterson said. "I've got to do what I'm told, especially by somebody like the Representative, if I wanna keep my job."

"What about your self-respect?" Clint asked.

Patterson hung his head.

"I lost that a long time ago." Then he looked up. "Can we go outside and do this? Or at least open the door. The stink . . ."

"Yeah, let's go outside."

Clint opened the door and let the sheriff step out ahead of him. That was why the bullet struck the lawman instead of him.

Patterson grunted and went down backward into Clint, who dragged him inside and slammed the door. When he checked the man, he saw it was no use, he was dead.

He left the lawman on the floor in front of the door— it would keep the door from being opened—and moved to a window. Gun in hand, he stared out and tried to see where the shot had come from. It was a single shot, fired accurately, which meant he was dealing with a professional. Could it be Frank Jeffrey?

"Frank!" he shouted. "Is that you out there?"

No answer.

"Frank!"

Still no answer. He either didn't want to give himself away, or it wasn't Jeffrey. And if it wasn't, then who was it? Who else did Representative Maxwell have on his payroll that could make a shot like that?

The only way to break this stand-off was to let himself be seen in a window, hope it would entice another shot so he could locate the shooter. He'd be taking a chance, since the shooter was obviously good, but once he had them located, he could take a shot of his own, or go out the back and try to circle around.

And, of course, there was always the possibility that the shooter was now gone, having done what he came to do. Clint found it hard to believe that the sheriff had been shot my mistake. Patterson had to be the chosen target.

Since that now made more sense to Clint than anything, he took the chance and stood up in front of the window.

Nothing.

Okay, maybe they were trying to entice him outside.

He decided to leave Patterson's body in front of the door and go out a rear window. Hopefully, there wasn't a second shooter watching the back. But first he walked to the fallen lawman and removed the badge from his shirt. Even in death, he didn't deserve to be wearing it.

Luckily, the back window had been knocked out a long time ago, so there was no glass to contend with. He climbed out, waiting for a shot and the impact of a bullet, but there was none. Apparently, there was one shooter.

Once outside, he executed a wide circle as he tried to figure where the shot might have come from. When he came to a stand of bushes, he crouched down and waited to see if anyone would try approaching the shack. He was patient, and waited a half hour. By that time, he was convinced that whoever had fired the shot was gone.

He moved in and searched the area he himself would have chosen to take a shot from, and found the ground had been trampled. The sound of the shot told him a rifle had been used, so he searched for an ejected shell, but the shooter had been expert enough to pick it up and take it away with him.

Eventually he walked back to the shack, but instead of trying to get the front door open, he simply mounted Eclipse and rode away. There was no harm in leaving the sheriff's body in there with the other three.

He decided to go and find Frank Jeffrey.

Chapter Forty-One

Clint rode Eclipse back to town, but when they got close enough, he dismounted and walked the Darley the rest of the way. Once again, he stopped behind the jailhouse and left Eclipse there while he went inside.

He went to the front window and looked out. He wanted to find Jeffrey, but he didn't want the people in town to know that he was back. He decided to try to keep to alleys and side streets.

First he wanted to go to the Riverboat Saloon to see if Jeffrey was there. He thought he could do that the back way.

He went out the back door, left Eclipse there and began working his way down the street. Then he used an alley to get to the main street. As he peered out, he saw he was across the street and just down from the Riverboat. He was going to have to leave the alley to cross over, but there was another alley directly across the way. He thought his best bet was just to walk across the street and down that alley. Maybe he had an exaggerated idea of how many people in town knew who he was.

He let some people walk by, and when it looked clear, he stepped out and started across the street. Nobody shouted, and nobody took a shot. When he got across the street he ducked into that alley, and took it to the rear of the Riverboat. The back door there was quite different from the back door of the jail. It was locked tight, and no amount of pressure from his shoulder would open it.

There were several windows, but judging from the soundness of the back door, they'd all be locked. He tried them anyway, and lo and behold, one of them was unlocked. The security of any building was only as strong as its weakest point.

He got his fingertips under the window and swung it open, then climbed inside and closed it. The light through the window showed him to be in the back storeroom. He moved to a doorway he figured would lead to the saloon floor. Sure enough, he was just behind the bar, with a view of the room. And Frank Jeffrey was sitting at the same table as before.

Clint stepped out and the bartender, Hank, immediately spotted him.

"You're a talented man," he said, "for somebody who's supposed to be out of town, you're in two places at one time."

"I'm just here to talk to Jeffrey."

"You want a beer while you're at it?"

"I'll take two."

Hank drew him two and Clint carried them over to Frank Jeffrey's table.

"I had a feeling you'd be back," Jeffrey said. "That's why I didn't follow when you rode out."

Clint sat, pushed one fresh beer across to Jeffrey, who drained the one he had and picked up the new one.

"Thanks," He sipped it. He held it in his right hand and Clint remembered he was left-handed.

"Somebody killed the sheriff a little while ago," Clint said, "You been here all morning?"

"Why ask me?" Jeffrey said. "Ask Hank. Or some of these others."

Clint looked around. It was early, but there were easily a dozen other men in the room.

"I can't pay them all to lie," Jeffrey said.

"Maybe not," Clint said, "but the Representative could."

"Not Hank," Jeffrey said. "He's his own man."

Clint looked over at the bartender, who was watching them while wiping glasses with an off-white rag. He had a feeling Jeffrey might be right, and he didn't lie. He thought and voiced the question at the same time.

"If not you, then why?"

Jeffrey shrugged.

"Somebody with a beef against the sheriff?" he asked. "Or do you think the bullet was meant for you."

"No," Clint said "It was one shot, real clean. It was meant for him."

"Well, I had nothin' against the sheriff."

"You've got nothing against me, either, Frank," Clint said, "but that's not going to stop you from trying to kill me."

"Kill you, definitely," Jeffrey said, "not try. And it's just a job."

"Right, a job."

"Why are you still here, anyway?"

"Initially, I thought it was to get the badge off the sheriff's chest," Clint said, "because he didn't deserve to wear it."

"But he's dead now, and you're still here."

"And now I think it's the Representative," Clint said. "I'd hate like hell to see him rise any higher in the U.S. government."

"So you're gonna stop him."

"I'm going to try."

"By killin' him?" Jeffrey asked.

"By proving he's behind the killings."

"I think you'd have a better chance at killin' him," Jeffrey said.

"But you're in the way."

Jeffrey sipped his beer and said, "There is that."

Chapter Forty-Two

"So where do we go from here?" Jeffrey asked.

"I guess that's up to you," Clint said. "I'm going after the Representative. You're being paid to stop me. Do you want to do it now?"

"Actually," Jeffrey said, "I haven't got the word yet from him."

"Then why don't we walk over to his office together," Clint said, "and see what he says? I'm sure he's there, waiting to hear if I'm gone."

"Okay," Jeffrey said, "why don't we?" He stood up, took one last, long pull on his beer, then pointed at the batwing doors. "After you."

"Oh no," Clint said, standing, "you first. I insist."

"I'm gonna go first," Jeffrey said, "because I know you won't shoot me in the back."

"Are you sure?"

"Very," Jeffrey said. "You just ain't the type."

Jeffrey headed for the doors, with Clint right behind him. He could feel that the man was relaxed, and believed what he said.

And why not? He was right.

***

When they got to the Representative's office door Jeffrey stopped and stepped aside. Clint walked up and opened the door without knocking. Then *he* stepped aside to allow Jeffrey to enter first.

There was an outer office, but the Representative did not seem to have a secretary or an assistant, so they went directly to his office door and Clint opened it.

Maxwell looked up from his desk, seemed surprised to see Clint, but composed himself quickly.

"Mr. Adams," he said, "to what do I owe—"

"Can it, Maxwell," Clint said, tossing Patterson's badge onto the man's desk, "your pet lawman's dead, so that makes four people you had killed for some reason only you know."

"What are you blabbering about?"

"Murder," Clint said. "I'm bringing a federal marshal in to arrest you for conspiracy to commit murder. All I need to find out is who actually did the deeds."

"How do I know you didn't?" Maxwell asked. "Between the two of us, which one has the reputation as a killer?"

"He's got you there," Jeffrey said, seemingly amused.

"The two of you may find this funny," Clint said, "but believe me, it won't be. Not when the federal marshal gets here. I'm headed for the telegraph office to send a message to Washington." He only hoped they'd agree to send a marshal into the territory of Wyoming.

As he left the office, he wondered if, in Washington, they were even aware that Maxwell was calling himself a Representative?

***

After Clint left, Frank Jeffrey looked at Maxwell. "So?"

"Do what I paid you to do."

Jeffrey nodded, and left the office.

Maxwell stood up, donned his jacket, and went out the back door.

***

"Clint!"

He turned around when Jeffrey called his name. They were still in front of Maxwell's office.

"I wondered if the would-be politician would send his lap dog after me."

Jeffrey laughed.

"Tryin' to get under my skin?" he asked. "It ain't gonna work."

"Then do what you've got to do Frank," Clint said. "I'm dead tired of this town."

"Not dead tired," Jeffrey said. "Just dead."

He drew, and was not nearly as fast as he thought he was. Clint had his gun out first, and put a bullet squarely in the center of Jeffrey's chest. It was too bad. He liked the man, but this wasn't the first time a man he liked gave in to the urge to try him—or was paid to.

He walked to where Jeffrey lay as people began to run over to see what had happened.

Clint leaned over Jeffrey, saw that the man was still alive, but knew it wasn't for long.

"Sorry, Frank," he said, and then Jeffrey died.

He stood, ejected the spent shell and replaced it. A group of men surrounded the fallen Jeffrey and recognized him.

One of them looked at Clint.

"You're the Gunsmith."

"That's right."

"So Jeffrey finally decided to try you?"

"That's what it looks like."

"Should I go and get the sheriff?" the man asked.

"You do that," Clint said.

He turned and went back to Maxwell's office.

Chapter Forty-Three

Maxwell was gone.

Clint found the back door, saw the buggy tracks in the dirt. There was only one place he could have been going.

Instead of heading back through the office and out the front door to deal with the crowd, Clint made his way along the back of the building, walked down the street so he could cross back to the jail.

Eclipse had obediently remained where he was, so Clint mounted up and started his ride back to Maxwell's ranch. He decided to take the man into custody and ride to the next town that had a sheriff. Hopefully, they'd listen to him there.

***

Maxwell rushed into his house, yelling "Simms!"

His man appeared quickly.

"What is it, sir?"

"Where's Helena?"

"In her room, I think."

"Well check," Maxwell said. "If she's there, tell her to come down."

"Yessir!"

As Simms ran up the stairs, Maxwell went into the living room area instead of his office. He had good brandy in a sidebar there, as well, and poured himself some.

"What's going on?" Helena asked, entering the room with Simms behind her.

"Wait a minute," he said. "Simms, go and find Hutch."

"Yes, sir."

As Simms left the house, Maxwell sat down on an armchair.

"Are you going to tell me what's going on?" she asked.

"Jeffrey went after Adams."

"Who killed who?" she asked.

"I don't know," he said. "I didn't want to find out. But if Adams killed him, then he'll be coming here, next."

"So it's all falling apart?"

"Not if I can help it," Maxwell said.

"Do you really think you're the one they'll put in charge if and when Wyoming is granted statehood?" she asked.

"I'm betting on it," he said. "And it's a big bet."

Simms came back in, with Hutchinson behind him.

"Yeah, boss?"

"How many men do we have who can handle a gun?"

"Boss, my men are cowboys, not gunfighters."

"They wear guns, don't they?"

"Some of them."

Maxwell pointed at Hutchinson's hip.

"You wear one! Can you use it?"

"When I have to. What do you have in mind?"

"Clint Adams may be on his way here. I need—"

"Oh, no," Hutchinson said. "That's where I draw the line. I'm the foreman, and my men are cowpokes. Ain't nobody here gonna go up against the Gunsmith for you."

"No matter how much I pay them?"

Hutchinson hesitated then said, "Well, we'd have to see how much money we're talkin' about . . ."

***

Clint reined in when he came within sight of the ranch. He wondered how many of Maxwell's cowhands the man would convince to pick up a gun? He decided to go in on foot, rather than ride in.

He dismounted, left Eclipse near a stand of Cottonwood trees, and headed for the ranch.

***

"Five," Hutchinson said to Maxwell. "That's all that would take the offer."

"Five," Maxwell said. "And you?"

"That makes six," Helena said. "Think that's enough?"

"It better be," Maxwell said. He looked at Hutch, "Put them out front. I want them to watch for him."

"Yessir."

As the man went to the door, Maxwell shouted, "And if Frank Jeffrey rides in, tell them not to shoot him!"

***

Clint saw the men spread out in front of the house. He counted six, recognized one of them as Hutchinson, the foreman. Four of them were wearing holstered guns, all of them were holding rifles.

He was more concerned about the rifles. Even a cowhand could be good with a rifle. He had to keep them from seeing him approach the house. He decided to try the back, see if Maxwell was smart enough—or had enough men—to cover the back.

When he got there, he saw no men. He decided the six in front were the only ones Maxwell had convinced—with money—to go up against him.

He started for the back door.

Chapter Forty-Four

The door was locked, but looking through the window he saw that it lead to the kitchen which, at the moment, was empty. He tried to force it, but the lock was too good. He was going to have to find another way in.

There were enough windows in back of the house that one had to be open. He kept trying them until, on the fourth, he found one he could force. He climbed in, saw that he was in a hallway that he recognized. It was right near Maxwell's office. From further down the hall, he could hear voices. Men, and a woman. It had to be Helena.

He worked his way down the carpeted hallway, peered into the office and saw that it was empty. As he got to the end of the hall, the voice became more discernible.

"The men are stationed outside, boss," he heard Hutchinson say. The man must have come in from outside.

"All right," Maxwell said, "you stay in here with us."

"Yes, sir."

The "us" must have been him, Helena, and probably his man, Simms.

Clint moved out of the hall, took a few steps, and entered the living room. Maxwell was pacing, holding a brandy snifter that was half full. Simms was standing off to one side, hands behind his back, Helena was seated on a sofa. Hutchinson turned, saw Clint, and started to go for his gun.

"Don't!" Clint snapped. "You'd never make it."

"He's right, Hutch," Helena said. "Don't do it."

Hutch looked at Helena and took his hand away from his gun. Helena's voice sounded as if she was the one in charge, which puzzled Clint.

"What the hell are you doin' here?" Maxwell demanded.

"I'm taking you in," Clint said. "Jeffrey confessed before he died that he was working for you."

"He's dead?" Maxwell said.

"Everybody's dead, Maxwell," Clint said. "You got them all, but you didn't get me, so I'm going to get you. Let's go."

"How do you expect to get me past those men out there?" Maxwell asked.

"Those men are cowpokes, not gunmen," Clint said. "They'll back off."

Maxwell looked at Hutch and Helena. It was Helena who spoke.

"He's right, William," she said, "Go with him."

"What?"

"He's got nothing on you," she said. "No matter where he takes you, the law there won't hold you."

"What if he just kills me on the way?" Maxwell demanded.

"He won't do that," Helena said. "He's not the type."

"Look," Maxwell said to Helena, "I brought you here to do a job—"

"Which we never got to," Helena said, "so I'll probably give you your money back."

"No need," Maxwell said. "Just take care of this situation, and we'll be even. In fact, I'll double your fee."

"Her fee?" Clint asked, confused. "What are you talking about?"

Maxwell looked at Clint.

"You've never heard of Helena Briscoe?"

"Not before yesterday," Clint said.

"Have you ever heard of Lady Hell?"

Clint stared at Maxwell.

"That's a myth," Clint said. "A female assassin who works for rich men."

"The Gunsmith is a myth," Maxwell said, "yet here you are."

Clint looked at Helena.

"So you were brought here to kill somebody?"

"Apparently," she said.

"Who?"

"We never did get to that," she said.

"So when you met me—"

"I was just hungry and looking for a table," she said. "And you looked interesting. Then, when I found out who you were, you got even more interesting."

"But then?"

"But then Mr. Maxwell, here, found out that I went to town, and he had a fit. See, he didn't want anybody knowing I was here. Didn't want anyone to see me, even though nobody knows what I look like."

"So he had everybody who saw you killed," Clint said.

"I suppose it seemed right, at the time," she said. "It did seem a little extreme to me, but . . ." She shrugged. ". . . he was payin' the bills."

"Wait," Clint said, "you killed them. All three?"

"Four," she said.

"The sheriff, too?"

"He seemed to be coming apart," she said.

"You're telling him too much!" Maxwell scolded.

"Relax, William," she said, "there are still things I haven't told him."

"Like what?" Maxwell demanded.

Helena smiled.

"Like what you enjoy doing for relaxation?"

Maxwell fell silent, his face turning red. Remembering her nails digging into his thighs, Clint had a rough idea what she was talking about.

"Well then," he said, "I guess we're all leaving."

Chapter Forty-Five

"Me?" Hutch asked. "Why am I goin'?"

"You're going outside to save the lives of your men."

"There are five men with guns out there," Maxwell said.

"He'll kill them all, William," Helena said.

He glared at her.

"Why didn't you tell me that before?"

She grinned.

"You didn't ask me."

Clint looked at Helena, who was dressed to ride, with Levis and boots. He was still dealing with the shock of finding out who she was. He felt like a fool for spending all that time looking for her, when he should've just left town.

"Do I have time to go upstairs and get my hat?" Helena asked.

"And a gun? No," Clint said. "We're leaving now."

"You'll never get me to the barn," Maxwell said.

"Watch me," Clint replied. He turned to Hutch. "Drop your gun, then go out there and tell your men to do the same."

"Adams." Hutch said, "the boss is payin' them a lot of money."

"Enough to die for?"

Hutch dropped his gun to the floor and said, "It just may be."

"Well," Clint said "do what you can. I'll watch from the window."

Hutch shrugged and headed for the door. Clint moved to the front window, while continuing to keep an eye on Maxwell and Helena. He doubted he had to wait for the Representative to make any kind of move, but he wasn't as sure about Helena, even though her hands were empty, and she wasn't wearing a gun. After all, they didn't call her Lady Hell for nothing.

"Both of you move over there together, so I can see you two."

They did as they were told, so he could look out the window and watch them easily.

He couldn't see Hutch, who was standing at the top of the steps, but he saw the five men come over to hear what he had to say. They stood quietly for a short time, then several of them started to shout something.

"They're not going to do it, are they? Nor going to put their guns down, are they?" Helena asked. "There's just too much money at stake."

"Damn it," Clint said.

"Money talks, Adams," Maxwell said, "it always has and it always will."

"You think I'm going out there and kill five men?" Clint asked.

"No," Maxwell said. "I think you're going out there so five men can kill you."

They heard the front door open and the foreman came back in. When he appeared, his shoulders were slumped. It was obvious what he was going to say.

"They're all willing to try for the money, Adams," he said. "I couldn't talk them out of it."

"I figured," Clint said.

"So now what?" Helena asked.

Clint looked directly at Maxwell.

"I should just kill you," he said. "Then there'd be nobody to pay them."

Maxwell looked shaken by that.

"Don't worry, William," Helena said. "He's not going do that."

Clint knew she was right. He couldn't shoot an unarmed man, not even to save the lives of five foolish men.

"What about you, Hutch?" Clint asked.

"Hey, my gun's on the floor, Adams," the foreman said.

"Okay then," Clint said, "I want you to go out the back, go to the barn and hitch up your boss's buggy. Can you walk it around to the back without the men seeing you?"

"I think so."

"Then do it," Clint said. "And don't run, because I'll find you."

"I understand."

Hutch left.

"They'll come after us," Maxwell said.

"It'll take them some time to saddle up," Clint said.

"We're not going to get so far ahead of them," Helena said. "Not in a buggy."

"I just need enough distance to pick them off with my rifle," Clint said.

"If you're going to kill them that way, why not just go out there and gun them down?" she asked.

"I'm not going to kill them," Clint said, "but I'll discourage them."

"You're crazy," Maxwell said. "You'll never get out of here."

"And where's your horse?" Helena asked.

"Don't worry, he's not far. We're going to walk the buggy to my horse, and then we'll all climb aboard and light out. If either one of you gives me trouble, I'll put a bullet in your leg—and you know I'll do that.

Chapter Forty-Six

While Hutch went for the buggy, Clint continued to watch the men out front, who seemed to be getting nervous about waiting. When Hutch returned with the news that the buggy was out back, Clint turned away from the window.

"If they decide to come in," Helena said, "you'll be forced to kill them all."

"Ranch hands don't come into the big house without being called for," Clint said. "They'll be waiting out there for a while. Come on."

He herded Maxwell, Hutch and Helena to the kitchen and out that door.

"What's the best way to go to avoid those men out front?" he asked Hutch.

"If you walk that way," the man said, pointing, "you'll be able to work your way behind the barn. The rest'll be easy."

"Hutch, you stay in the house for at least another hour," Clint said. "I'm not going to tie you up, but—"

"Don't worry, Adams," the foreman said, "I'm not looking to be a hero."

"All right," Clint said to Maxwell and Helena. "Helena, get in the buggy, and Maxwell, you get in front and walk that horse—and keep it and you quiet!"

Looking uncomfortable, Maxwell took the horse's head and started leading it. He was wearing one of his dark suits, but did not have a hat on.

They walked the buggy the way Hutch had told them, and managed to get around the barn without being seen. Clint figured the rest of the hands, knowing something was going to happen, were in the bunkhouse, where it was safe.

When they reached the Cottonwood trees where Clint had left Eclipse, he mounted up, and told Maxwell to get in the buggy. The man did so, and made no move to take the reins from Helena.

"All right, let's move out," Clint said.

"Where to?" she asked.

"We're heading for Billings," Clint said. "There should be a lawman there worth his salt."

"You think so, huh?" Maxwell asked, as Helena got the buggy going. "I don't know why I'm worried. I'll probably be back home by tomorrow night."

"We'll see about that, Maxwell," Clint said.

***

It was a day's ride to Billings, and since they had gotten a late start they were going to have to camp for the night. They stopped in a clearing and he had them step down from the buggy.

"You stop for the night and my men will catch up," Maxwell said.

"Your men aren't coming, Maxwell," Clint replied. "Time to give it up. We're going to start a fire."

"What about the horses?" Helena asked.

"I'll take care of them after the fire's going, and I tie the two of you up."

Helena and Maxwell exchanged glances.

"All right, Clint," Helena said, "it's time to stop all this. Just let us go and we'll go back to Split Rail. You can just . . . be on your way."

Clint looked at the two people facing him, didn't see where either could have a weapon.

Maxwell moved away from Helena, and that's when Clint knew she was going to make some kind of move.

"Helena—"

Her hand whipped out and he felt a sting in his left shoulder. Without hesitation, he drew and fired just as her hand was coming up again. The bullet struck her in the chest, between her breasts. Something whizzed past his ear as he dropped down to one knee.

"Jesus!" Maxwell snapped.

Clint stood up as Helena fell onto her back. He looked, saw a small piece of metal sticking in his chest. He moved his gun to his left hand and kept it trained on Maxwell while pulling the blade from his skin with his right. It was a small knife, maybe three inches long. Undoubtedly the thing that went past his ear was another one.

"You're fast," Maxwell said, "but I didn't know you were that fast. I—I never even saw you draw."

"Just stand still, Maxwell," Clint said. "Don't make me kill you."

"You killed her," Maxwell said. "You killed Lady Hell."

"She didn't leave me much choice."

Clint walked to her and crouched down. He patted her down, then felt her sleeves. Inside the right one was a contraption that held a third blade. She'd thrown two.

"Ingenious," Clint said.

"That was only one of her toys, but now you'll never see the others."

"She killed two people this way, strangled another," Clint said. He knew she was strong, because he'd felt it when they were together.

"She was a killing machine," Maxwell said, "and more."

Clint stood up, looking down at her sadly.

"What now?" Maxwell asked. "Why don't you just let me go?"

"First," Clint said, "you're going to bury Helena. Then we'll make camp. In the morning we'll head out."

"To Billings?"

"No," Clint said. "There'd be too much explaining to do. We're going to change direction. We're going to Denver."

"Why the hell are we going to Colorado?"

"Two reasons," Clint said. "I want to take you out of Wyoming Territory, and I'll have less explaining to do there."

"Why's that?"

"There's a federal marshal named Custis Long. He knows me, and he'll listen. Now start digging."

"With what?" Maxwell demanded. "I don't have a shovel."

Clint pointed his gun at the man and said, "Well then, I guess you'll have to use your hands."

Coming August 27, 2019

THE GUNSMITH
450
The Ambush of Belle Starr

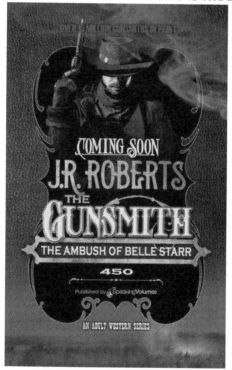

**For more information
click here:** www.SpeakingVolumes.us

On Sale Now!

THE GUNSMITH
448

For more information
visit: www.SpeakingVolumes.us

On Sale Now!

THE GUNSMITH *series*
Books 430 – 447

**For more information
visit:**

Coming Soon!

Lady Gunsmith 7
Roxy Doyle and the James Boys

For more information
visit: www.SpeakingVolumes.us

On Sale Now!

Lady Gunsmith *series*
Books 1-6

**For more information
visit:**

On Sale Now!

ANGEL EYES *series*
by Award-Winning Author
Robert J. Randisi (J.R. Roberts)

For more information
visit:

On Sale Now!

MOUNTAIN JACK PIKE *series*
by Award-Winning Author
Robert J. Randisi (J.R. Roberts)

For more information
visit: www.SpeakingVolumes.us

Sign up for free and bargain books

Join the Speaking Volumes mailing list

Text
ILOVEBOOKS
to 22828 to get started.

Message and data rates may apply.

Made in the USA
Coppell, TX
13 April 2020